DEAD
OF WINTER

SAM HOOKER ⚔ LAURA MORRISON
ALCY LEYVA ⚔ CASSONDRA WINDWALKER
DALENA STORM ⚔ N.J. EMBER
DANIEL BUELL ⚔ TIFFANY MEURET

Foreword by 2018 Bram Stoker Nominated Author Monique Snyman
Edited by Lindy Ryan

ISBN Print: 978-1-64548-059-4
ISBN Ebook: 978-1-64548-060-0

Cover Design and Interior Formatting
by Qamber Designs and Media
Edited by Lindy Ryan

Published by Black Spot Books
An imprint of Vesuvian Media Group

OTHER ANTHOLOGIES
BY BLACK SPOT BOOKS

A Midnight Clear
Edited by Lindy Ryan

TABLE OF CONTENTS

Foreword, Monique Snyman

Acknowledgements
About the Authors

DEDICATIONS

For my sister, Mary, whose sense of humor is just depraved enough to appreciate what I've written.
— Sam Hooker

For every banished dragon who still misses the sky, every page-caged soul. — Cassondra Windwalker

To anyone who needs it. There is hope.
— Dalena Storm

To my parents, who have supported me every step of the way. — Daniel Buell

To all the dark spots in my mind and the people who live there. — Alcy Leyva

For my boys, whom will be directed to this story when they inevitably ask, "Just how stressed were you during the quarantine?" — Tiffany Meuret

In loving memory of Kianna Tubbs, Nathaniel Mosby, and Nathan Weller. Beautiful souls gone too soon.
— N. J. Ember

To Katie. — Laura Morrison

FOREWORD

MONIQUE SNYMAN

As the air turns crisp and the trees become barren, many look at the world through rose-tinted glasses. Oh, what wondrous magic awaits us all! Decorations and overflowing shelves filled with bright and shiny trinkets to buy and gift to those you love. Snowflakes drifting on the wind, a white blanket to cover the gray concrete we've all become so accustomed to throughout the year, cheery holiday greetings and time spent with family and friends. Yes, the Winter Spirit lives in most of us then.

But what is the Winter Spirit if not merely an elemental *idea* brought to life by sentimental fools?

We, as humans, have turned winter into the most glorious time of the year, when in truth it remains the most unforgiving season of all.

We conveniently forget about the smog trapped in the cities as the cold descends, we forget about the lonely souls who have nobody to spend their holidays with, we forget about those left out as the weather rages. It simply doesn't fit the picture perfect winter we've been sold by marketing companies. We forget, because we don't want to remember how difficult things can be without the luxuries we've surrounded ourselves with to keep the long, dark nights at bay.

Not too long ago, however, our views on winter were different. Oral traditions told of the hardships that came along with the heavy snowfall and a lingering winter. Folklore warned of demons lurking in the shadows, searching for disobedient children. There were more to fear back then, yes, but for the Winter Spirit, time has no meaning and our ignorance won't save us.

A darkness lingers at this time of year, cloaked by that sparkling white blanket and those shiny gift-wrapped presents. Sometimes, the darkness is invisible, born in one's mind or lurking just on the edges of traditions, other times it is a menacing force that demands to be noticed.

The type of darkness you'll meet in your lifetime depends, I suppose, on whether you're in the wrong place at the wrong time or not …

In *Dead of Winter*, eight authors explore this darkness, these often-overlooked horrors that come along with the Winter Spirit. Some of these journeys may seem familiar, perhaps you've even come across a similar wintery experience in your travels, but others will be new. New and terrifying, no doubt. From Christmas cheer, which quickly turns into Christmas fear, to hearing and ignoring Death's call. Get lost in tales of madness, brought on by what feels like an unending cold, and follow trails to find those lost and frightening things that should never have existed in the first place. Through mirrors we find new worlds and other selves, through time we hear agonizing screams that traveled through millennia to knock on your door. Vengeance and punishments, close calls and sacrifice. *Dead of Winter* has something for everyone!

The Winter Spirit is here, dear reader, and with it comes these eight cautionary tales to help stave off the icy chill, for winter is intolerant to those who are unprepared and reckless, and the Winter Spirit has no mercy to spare.

So heed these authors' warnings, one and all: Take off those rose-tinted glasses and see what lies beneath the pretty lies. Scrape away at the veneer we've been sold and truly see what is watching you, just waiting for the perfect moment to strike.

THE WATCHFUL CROW

SAM HOOKER

C rime was easy. Teaching crows about pockets was the hard part.

Orville had been out of the game for decades. He was older than he looked, and he didn't look young.

There was a clamor of black feathers at his shoulder followed by a clink. A quarter.

"Not bad," said Orville. He offered up a whole peanut in its shell. The bird snatched it with haste, flying away before the old man had a chance to change his mind. Not that he ever had. Orville paid his murder well, especially top earners like Mister Gleam. Coins were elusive to crows, always at the bottoms of pockets and purses, under keys and pocketknives. It was a rare crow like Mister Gleam who knew how to think like a kingfisher. Dart in fast and deep, get away with the shiny fish before it even knew it had a reason to be afraid. So quick the water didn't have a chance to get him wet.

Most crows were more like Mister Gumwrapper. Day-old breadcrumbs kept them fed, but still hungry. Orville made a show of giving peanuts to Mister Gleam. Earn for the boss, reap the rewards.

A biting chill ripped through the clear blue sky. Orville

gathered his scarf a little higher around his neck. He'd moved south to get away from the brutal winters, but they followed him. Either that or the ignominy of age was mocking him. It didn't take much to chill his bones these days, especially in the short days of December.

At least he didn't have to deal with snow anymore. That was good. Crows flew south to get away from snow, and they were all the friends he had left. This was a lazy murder, found a sweet spot where they could hang around all year. Cold, but not freeze-you-solid cold.

Another great flapping at his shoulder and a thunk in his lap. The sizzling sound of a silver chain coming to rest. Orville looked down at the pocket watch. Who carried pocket watches anymore?

"Very nice," said Orville. He opened the bag of peanuts wide, expecting Mister Gleam to dive in, but the bird simply hopped onto the bench rail and watched him. That was odd. Orville was an expert on crows in his own estimation, but he'd be buggered if he could suss out what was happening behind that black stare.

"Er, hi," came a voice from behind him. Orville flinched. No one had snuck up on him in years. It was a woman walking a pit bull. Leggings, riding boots, scarf, and puffer vest—the woman, not the dog. She and Orville were wearing the same fedora. She looked like she'd just returned from a Starbucks safari.

The dog had a name tag shaped like a bone. Orville thought "Popcorn" was a strange name for a dog made entirely of muscles.

"Hello," said Orville. The watch disappeared into his coat pocket like a magic trick. A single fluid movement he'd perfected over a lifetime of cons and grifts. Still, her eyes darted down at the motion. It was the smoothest way he could have possibly made the interaction more awkward.

She nodded to Mister Gleam. "He a friend of yours?"

"Business associate," Orville admitted. He reluctantly drew

the watch back from his pocket. "This was yours, I presume?"

"Thanks," she said, relief washing over her face. The watch disappeared back into Orville's pocket as she reached for it, sending the tide of her relief washing back out.

"I asked if it was yours," said Orville. "Possession is nine-tenths of the law, you know."

She cocked an eyebrow. "You really want to have a conversation about the law?"

It wasn't a threat. Not yet. Orville was a connoisseur of threats. This, at best, was an inquiry aspiring to warn. The next few moments would determine whether he got to keep the first pocket watch he'd lifted since "somebody lifted my pocket watch!" wasn't a weird thing to say.

His heart fluttered in his chest. This was the knife's edge, where life happened. The air was crisp and sweet. One wrong step and she'd call the cops, or maybe she'd let Popcorn do the dirty work, though that seemed unlikely. As the moment wore on, the dog's dopey smile seemed to make sense of his name.

It was a tense situation, but not dangerous. For an old thief spending his winter years teaching birds the trade, manageable peril was a precious thing.

"What's a young gal doing with a pocket watch? Don't you have an app for that on your phone?"

"What's it to an old codger and his thieving birds?" She was looking at Mister Gleam, who sat patiently, unlike the rest of his murder. They were stalking bugs on the lawn or making big, lazy circles overhead, looking for their next marks.

"She's right, you know," Orville sang to Mister Gleam. "You just might be capable of proper thievery." He turned back to the young woman. "If there's one of these birds capable of the real deal, it's Mister Gleam here."

"That's great, I guess." If she was trying to conceal her agitation, she was no good at it. "Can I please have my watch back?"

"Please." Orville smiled, letting the word swirl around on his tongue. "I wasn't sure young people knew that word anymore."

3

"That's a coincidence."

"What's a coincidence?"

"My word-of-the-day email was 'sanctimony.' I definitely won't forget it now."

Orville scowled. He had no use for people who were smarter than him.

Amber was starting to creep into the western horizon. The wind picked up. The days were short this time of year, and the night air cut right through old men. Orville knew his arthritis would punish him if he didn't head home right then, but he decided to risk it. How often did pretty girls stop and talk to gnarled ex-cons? It was flattering, even if he had to steal her watch to get the ball rolling.

"Ask me how I do it," he said.

"How you do what?"

"The birds," said Orville. What else would he have meant? A hundred years ago, a guy who taught a crow to lift someone's watch would draw a crowd. Nowadays it wasn't even good enough for a "wow!" These Millennials and their smart phones.

"I read an article about crows not too long ago," she said. Her phone appeared in her hand as if it had been there the whole time.

Some magic trick, Orville thought.

"Yeah," she said, reading something that confirmed her memory. "They can use primitive tools, remember faces—there was this one guy who watched crows putting nuts on crosswalks so the cars would crack them, then waiting for the walk light to collect their reward."

"I know how smart the crows are, honey." Orville flashed her a decades-old charming smile. It hadn't aged as well as he thought. She flashed back a smirk that told him how amused she wasn't.

"Ugh, Millennials." Orville rolled his eyes.

"Okay, Boomer," she quipped. "I was born in 1998, so I'm Gen Z."

"And I was born before the Baby Boomers. No sense of humor, eh? Your dog's smiling, maybe he's the conversationalist?"

"She's not my dog. I'm just walking her. Or I would be, if some old man's bird hadn't stolen my watch."

"He's not my bird," said Orville. "He's my business associate."

"If you say so."

"So, you're a dog walker?"

"Something like that." She sighed with impatience. "Gig economy, you know how it is. Wait, no, you probably don't."

"I might know more about it than you think," said Orville. He knew he'd turn out to be the smart one. Maybe he had a use for her after all. "Doing whatever it takes to get by? Yeah, I know a thing or two about that. I robbed a bank six months after the Great Depression got underway."

She laughed out loud. "Pull the other one. That would have been 90 years ago! You're old, but you're not that old."

"Thanks." He tried not to take it personally, but Orville was sensitive about his looks. Guys who grew up handsome usually are. He'd lost everyone he'd known over the years, including that Dapper Dan in the mirror.

"Seriously, were you still in diapers?"

"I was twenty-six," Orville barked, louder than he'd intended. He regretted that. It didn't do to shout at people unless you were sticking a gun in their face. Then it was expected. Only a real psychopath would stick a gun in your face, smile, and ask politely for everything in the register.

Her eyes narrowed as she tried to make sense of the math. Orville thought she looked thinner, but dismissed the thought. They'd only just met. Not enough time for her to drop a few pounds.

"You were born in 1904?" Her voice lilted in disbelief.

"1903," he corrected her. "The heist was a week before my birthday. What a party that was! Girls, booze—prohibition was all but dead by then, didn't take someone as savvy as me to catch a crate of whiskey falling off a truck."

She was about to call bullshit when Mister Gleam interrupted. He cawed three times, his beady expression fixed on Orville.

Popcorn barked. Maybe in surprise, or maybe it was a warning. Either way, it was a powerful reminder that there were teeth behind her carefree smile, and she knew how to use them.

"Easy," said the woman.

Mister Gleam turned to lock eyes with her during the silence that fell. Crows were smart, though not great conversationalists. Still, he seemed to have something to say.

"I should be going," she said after a while. She held her hand out to Orville. "It'll be dark soon."

"Don't let me keep you," he replied. He made no move to return the watch.

She stood there, wearing a threadbare mask of patience.

"Ugh," she sighed. Her outstretched hand flashed near her purse, and her phone was in it. "This is ridiculous."

"What are you going to do?"

"CAW!" insisted Mister Gleam. He hopped across Orville's lap to perch on the other arm of the bench, closer to the woman. They stared at each other again, the moment dragging silence back over them. Pink crept across the first amber hues of the evening like a bloodstain on a brass doorknob.

"You look tired," said Orville, as though the silence were his to break. He knew it wasn't. He knew he was being rude, and that was half the point. He wanted to keep her off balance, make her forget she was going to call the cops to report him, and for what? Accepting a gift from a crow? Sure, she said the watch was hers, but could she prove it?

"You do, too," she replied, not as mad as she should have been. She squinted at Orville as if seeing him for the first time. She did look thinner, he was sure of it.

"Not me. I'm a night owl. Always have been. Goes with the trade."

"No, that's hours tired. You're years tired." She looked to the west. The sun was setting on the horizon, partially obscured by a heavy, gray cloud. Her eyes shifted back to Orville for a moment, then back to the sun again, then back to Orville.

"You're not lying, are you?"

Orville put one hand over his heart, raised the other next to his head. "Every word I've spoken has been true. From a certain perspective."

Her head leaned to one side. Her neck crackled like wolves chasing a rabbit over bubble wrap.

"Would you be interested in a trade?" she asked.

"What've you got?"

"The watch," said the woman. "You can keep it."

"I've already got the watch." Orville gave her a wink that was entirely out-of-place outside of dive bars.

"I said I'd let you keep it."

Popcorn gave a quiet woof. Orville understood what it meant. He was a connoisseur of threats, after all.

"I don't know," said Orville. He was certain he'd queued up something to follow that, but for the life of him, he couldn't remember what. He reached for the watch, or at least he'd meant to, but his hand didn't move.

He wanted to give it back to her. He'd had his fun, but this was getting weird. Century-old instincts were screaming at him to disappear from this, whatever this was. You walk away when it doesn't feel right. She was even thinner now than she'd been a moment ago.

On second thought, why shouldn't he keep it? He'd earned it. It sang to him. One long, steady note humming directly into his soul. It was like blood flowing back into an arm that he'd slept on funny, warm and soothing.

"What do you want?" asked Orville, suddenly very aware of his heartbeat.

"Truth."

"About what?"

"About you," she said. "Not the truth, I doubt you'd know it if you saw it. But you know your truth, and I'd like to hear it.

Do we have a deal?"

Do we have a deal? There was a vile phrase. He'd heard it a million times, the siren song of cops and criminals alike. It sounded a lot like "let's work together," but it really meant "give me your word, so if you break it I get to break your legs." Orville avoided deals like the plague. He'd have to put on his old charm, dazzle her with the old sidestep.

He smiled and winked to buy himself a moment, then leaned toward her conspiratorially and said, "Deal."

What? How had she done that? Witchcraft, probably. Orville was the bamboozler, not the mark! Especially not to a Millennial—or whatever she called herself—on her tiptoes and barely out of diapers.

No, wait. Her face was young, but there was something else. Something older. Reincarnation? Hogwash. Everybody knew there was no such thing. But did she?

She smiled, her gaunt cheeks going so tight Orville worried they might crack.

"Look, I'm sorry about the misunderstanding," he wheedled. He dangled the watch in front of her. "I was just having a laugh. Here, please take it. I don't want to keep you."

"We had a deal," she sang. He'd heard that tune before, from detectives who were surprised to see him among suspects for a bootleg run. Sure, they were.

"Deals were meant to be …" What? Broken? Renegotiated? Picked apart by oily lawyers? Any of those would have worked, but the only thing he could think to say was, "Honored."

So he talked. He told her at length about growing up in the heartland. About losing his father to the Great War and his mother to Spanish Flu in the same year. About hitching out to the west coast, working as a fruit picker, and learning the art of the grift.

"There was the fella, Jed," said Orville. "We met in the orange groves in the picking season, must've been 1919. I came off the back of a pickup truck without a penny to my name, starving to death in true bumpkin fashion. He was the only one who was nice to me. We joined up with the circus after picking season. Decent paying jobs were slim pickings in those days. It was fun for a while, but damn those carnies for thieves and bastards. We had to light out of there one night with nothing but the clothes on our backs."

She watched him with the unblinking intensity of a statue. It unnerved Orville. Young people didn't pay attention to the elderly. Orville hadn't maintained eye contact with anyone for more than ten seconds since Clinton was in the White House.

He looked up into the reddening sky to avoid her gaze. "Anyway, we ended up on the streets of Chicago, doing what we called odd jobs. There were plenty of those available if you knew who was hiring, and 'odd' didn't begin to cover some of them."

"Something's wrong." Her voice was dry and cracked like her skin. Her eyes were turning dark, fading back into the shadows of her brow.

"What is it? Do you need to go?" Orville thrust the watch toward her, casting the ghost of his aloofness to the frigid wind. He stared at her in desperation, willing her to take the damned thing and leave him be.

"No," she replied in a cough. "Something went wrong. With one of your odd jobs."

Orville sagged. He drew his hand back to his lap, the watch seeming very heavy in it. He forced half a smile.

"Lucky guess," he groaned. He opened his mouth, hesitated, closed it again.

"You want to ask me something." It wasn't a question. It seemed the darkness coming over her provided a window into Orville's soul. That flustered him. He was no good at directness. The truth, in his experience, was best approached at angles.

"What's happening right now?" Orville's voice quavered. It was small, nearly lost in the wind that whipped between them.

"You owe me the truth," she replied. She leaned in toward him with a squint. "Tell me about the bartender."

A chill ran down Orville's spine. To be fair, that had been a regular occurrence of late. For men of his venerability, "sweater weather" started when the mercury dipped below 80 degrees.

"How did you know about that?"

"You told me. No, you're going to tell me. Sorry, the sun's almost set. Time's all starting to run together. Wait, is it a bartender or a banker?"

"One of each." Orville reckoned there was no sense being coy. There was no way she could have known all of this. It was 1930! Everyone involved but Orville was dead.

"Everyone but you," she said, her eyes trailing across the horizon, focused on nothing.

"You already know," said Orville, "don't you?"

"Most of it," she replied. "But you still need to tell me."

"You want me to tell you what you already know?" Women, he thought, rolling his mind's eye.

"Names, dates," she said. "Those are just facts. What you owe me is truth."

Maybe she was a cop. He knew better than to ask. Despite what passes for common knowledge on TV, they don't have to tell you.

"The truth," Orville sighed. What was the truth? He kept his best lies next to the truth, pressed up against them. Cleanly separating one from the other would have been quite a feat. The moment had lived and died nearly a century ago.

"Say it," she said. Her voice was hollower, like she was talking up to him from the bottom of a well. Her hair hung limp, the bitter wind steering clear of it. "The thing you can't put into words. Just say it. We're dying to know."

Orville looked at Popcorn. The color had drained out of her. Her perpetual joyful expression remained, mocking him with carefree delight. She was the idiot void staring back at him.

"I died on my birthday." The words fell out of Orville single-file. "Or I should have. But death … missed."

"Death doesn't miss," said the husk of the woman. In the

purpling gloom, her skin had gone the color of milk. Her gaze offered no malice, just the promise of inevitability. Orville wouldn't have found comfort in the distinction had he tried, which he didn't.

"Not usually." Orville sighed. "Just me. I stepped aside and it took Jed instead."

There was more Orville wanted to say about that, but when he opened his mouth, nothing came out. Perhaps it was guilt. Perhaps it was instinct. Never tell the cops more than they need to hear. He sat there with his mouth open in the evening chill until his teeth ached before resigning himself to silence.

"That's not the way this works." The well of her voice reverberated in the gloom.

"Oh, no?" He hadn't had the upper hand for a while, and the little spark of indignation warmed him. It felt good. Who was she, this girl, this child whose visage was death? He was an old man when she cut her first teeth!

"You asked me for the truth," Orville shot back at her. "Why bother, if you already know it?"

"Truths collide, Orville." Was she breathing? Orville couldn't tell. "Few truths hold as much weight as death. It comes for us all, and all appointments are kept."

"Well, you asked for the truth and you got it," Orville barked.

Popcorn growled. Orville flinched.

"You'd better keep a hold of your dog." Or else what?

"She's not my dog."

Orville clenched his teeth in fury. Getting caught in a lie was one thing, but truths are sacred when you've only got a handful of them to your name. His fists shook. How dare she ask for truth and dismiss it?

"What are you, anyway?"

"Irish," she said. "On my dad's side."

"You know that's not what I meant."

"You mean it's not the truth you wanted to hear."

"There's a fair bit of that going around."

She turned to Popcorn. "I may as well tell him."

Orville missed whether Popcorn reacted. He was distracted by a long, gleeful cawing from Mister Gleam. The crow hopped back and forth on the arm of the bench, dancing a little jig on his perch.

"You talking to your dog now?" asked Orville, scrambling for a little control over the conversation that was getting weirder by the second.

"The world is dying," she replied. "Descending into darkness by inches. Can't you see it all around you? We no longer live in a time of plenty. We have to work the gig economy, squeeze a few bucks out of everything we do if we hope to see another sunrise. That's why I take these little jobs."

"What job? What are you talking about?"

Mister Gleam cawed and cackled. She looked at him with a sunken stare.

"He doesn't believe in reincarnation," she said to the bird. "Too bad. If he did, he'd have figured it out by now."

Orville kept quiet. He hadn't figured out what her game was, but maybe if he waited long enough, she'd waste away to nothing and he wouldn't have to find out. He'd rather lay awake wondering tonight, if it meant living to see another day.

"It's a curious case," she said, "now that I can see the whole shape of it. The banker emptied his pistol into you. Just you. He was a good shot."

Orville winced. A discreet doctor had pulled six slugs out of him and stitched him up. He hadn't thought about his scars in years, but now they itched. He'd been sitting in the speakeasy next to Jed, toasting his birthday and their good fortune.

"I did all the talking with the banker," said Orville, digging into a long-buried memory for the details. "Jed was just muscle. He didn't have to say anything. He had this look that could just about break your legs on its own."

"You ruined him," she said. "The banker."

Orville shook his head. "He dug his grave himself. Fella

with access to all that cash gets carried away betting on the ponies? Our employer collected marks like him. Rough him up a couple of times—nothing serious, just to get the desperation flowing—then we come in and throw him a life preserver. He opens up the vault for me and Jed, looks the other way for a minute, and poof! His debt gets wiped out. Magic. We even gave him a little taste of the proceeds, invited him to the speakeasy for my birthday. How'd that ruin him?"

"The police went to his house," she told him without inflection, like she was reading the news on TV. "They questioned his wife."

"I never knew that."

"Had he gotten home a minute earlier, they'd have arrested him. Instead, he panicked. His mind turned to revenge."

One long caw came from Mister Gleam, then a staccato cackle.

"He went to the speakeasy," she continued.

"Yeah," said Orville. He scratched the small of his back. "I know the tune, you can quit humming."

They watched in silence as the last crescent of the sun disappeared behind the horizon. Purple began fading to indigo behind blackening clouds.

"How did you do it?" asked the altogether skeletal figure of the woman. Her own personal darkness swirled around her like it was a living thing, although "living" was probably the wrong word, given the context.

"That's my last card," said Orville. "Not sure I want to play it yet."

"You don't have long," she said, sending a chill up Orville's spine. "I'm only curious. You can keep it to the end, but you can't take it with you."

"I imagine that goes for the watch, too. Why should I give you the last of my truth for nothing?"

"Fair enough," she said. "Your last truth for the rest of the story."

"I know the rest of the story. A creepy hipster murders an old man in the park. Sound about right?"

She shook her head. "You died a long time ago, you just weren't collected. Think of this as correcting the ledger. But you don't have the whole story. You don't know about Jed."

The pang in his heart was only guilt, but he thought it might kill him anyway. For years after that fateful night, he felt constant remorse for what he'd done to Jed. As the years went by, Jed occurred to him less and less. Each time, his guilt was all the heavier for his forgetfulness.

"I think we were with the circus for three years," said Orville. "We were in Tennessee early one spring when the bottom dropped out. We hunkered down in the tents for nearly a week waiting out that godawful rain. I played a lot of cards. Jed had his nose stuck in a book."

"*The Count of Monte Cristo*."

An hour ago, Orville would have been surprised she knew that. Now that she was nothing more than a conversational pile of bones, he doubted he'd live long enough to be surprised again.

"*The Count of Monte Cristo*," he confirmed. "Jed thought literature made him educated. He was right, but I was the one who got an education that week. There was this fortune teller, really pretty gal, had a deck of cards. Not tarot cards, just an old set of Bicycles. She and I were playing one night, and I won big."

"Not money," she said.

"Better," said Orville. "That fortune teller—Delilah was her name—she was older than I was, and to hear her talk you'd think she'd looped the world a hundred times. One lifetime wasn't enough for all of that. She must've had a dozen. It was her idea to bet secrets. She collected them, that's what she told me. I knew she had a good hand when she said she wanted to go all in. She never bluffed.

"So there we were, our darkest secrets in the balance. She throws down a full house, queens and sixes. You should've seen her eyes when my four jacks hit the table."

"You cheated."

"I didn't, usually, but something told me her darkest secret was worth the risk. I'd cuffed a pair of knaves, and she dealt me two more. What would you have done?"

"Not stolen the cards."

"Live a little," said Orville. He winced, but if she was offended, her perpetual grin didn't let on. "Anyway, she was true to her word. She gave me the secret of death."

"And what is the secret of death?"

"Everyone's got an end, and if you're quick, you can get someone else to take your place."

"That's the secret of death?" She seemed amused, like she'd just asked a five-year-old how old his father was.

Orville folded his arms in a huff. He stared off into the black sky for a moment, then his expression softened. He laughed.

"The con man's curse," he said. "My lies sound so much like the truth, even I can barely tell them apart. But yeah, that's the honest truth. And unfortunately for poor old Jed, I was quick when that coward shot me in the back."

"Why him? The speakeasy was full of people, why Jed?"

Orville gave her a sidelong glance. "You really don't know, do you?"

She steepled her bony hands at her chin. "Death isn't accustomed to being cheated, Orville."

"Referring to oneself in the third person has never been cool."

"Oh, I'm not Death. There's no capital-D Death. Think of me as your Uber."

"There's that gig economy," Orville mumbled.

She shrugged. "It's a living."

"Ha!" It felt good to laugh, but he didn't have many more coming. This was it, wasn't it? And the last laugh is always on you.

"The people in our lives," Orville said slowly, reaching for the right words, "the paths we walk, the experiences we share. That's where our souls overlap...or something like that. I don't really understand it myself. By then, Jed and I had spent every day of a decade together. We were practically the same fella. When lowercase-D death bore down on me, I just sort of stepped aside."

She smiled at him, not that she could have done anything else. Orville tried to smile back, but he didn't have it in him. He'd betrayed the best friend he'd ever had, and even the better part of a century couldn't wash that stain from his conscience. But even against the imminent call of fate, Orville was human to a fault. He wanted to live. 117 years was far more than most people got, and what did he have to live for? He hadn't gotten close to anyone, not the way he'd been with Jed.

"Just my murder," he mused aloud.

"You died a long time ago," she corrected him.

"I meant the birds," said Orville. "You know a flock of crows is called a murder? They're the only ones who'll know I'm gone. Mister Gleam, here, he gets it. He's the closest friend I've had since …"

Mister Gleam was looking at Orville. Staring at him. He knew crows could be patient, but they didn't stare. Like most wild things, they were constantly on the lookout for predators, prey, or a statue that didn't have any shit on it. Even Mister Gleam, who was particularly bright for a crow, kept his beak swiveling all day long. Not the sort of bird who'd be caught unawares.

"Jed?" Orville's voice was barely a whisper.

"I wondered if I'd have to draw you a picture," said Orville's death. "You believe in reincarnation yet?"

Orville had never seen a crow dance an Irish jig, but he'd seen Jed do it dozens of times. Give the man a pull off the moonshine, belt out a tune, and the fire in his belly shot straight to his feet. Mister Gleam hopped from one foot to the other, just like Jed.

"Well, I'll be damned," Orville chuckled. "I suppose that's twice we've been together until the end, eh, old buddy?"

Jed cackled again. He craned his neck toward Orville and crowed long and hard, his beak open wide. It took a moment, but the old man realized Jed wasn't laughing with him.

"It's time to go." Orville's death was on her feet.

"Hang on a minute," Orville pleaded. "Come on, Jed, you're not still sore about that, are you? It was decades ago!"

"Caw!"

"You took those decades from him," she translated. "Those years should have been his."

"Says who?"

"Says him, for one. I'm not here to judge, but I doubt anyone else would see it your way."

"Nonsense," said Orville. "This is America! Plenty of people would see it my way. I worked hard to have this life. I'm the personification of the American dream!"

"You've got the hubris," his death granted him, "not to mention the disregard for the consequences."

"Consequences?" Orville's voice quavered. He'd never had much truck with religion, in part because his parents had thumped so much of it into him. For the first time in years, visions of fire and brimstone danced in his head.

"You didn't think you could cheat death forever, did you? Or that there wouldn't be a reckoning? You've only managed to delay the inevitable, and the late fees have piled up. So to speak."

"But you came back, Jed!" He searched the crow's glossy black eyes for a hint of compassion. "Not as a man, I guess, but now you can fly. And you don't have to wear pants. You always hated pants."

The crow blinked. He stared at Orville, a calculating glare brimming with daggers.

"This is revenge." The realization chilled his blood. "I thought I had a friend in you, but you just wanted to get even."

Jed danced and cackled at that.

"He thought he had a friend in you, too," said Orville's death. "How'd that work out for him?"

Orville buried his face in his hands. He looked miserable, on the verge of tears, but none came. Instead he let out a great sigh.

"Is it going to hurt?" he asked his death.

"Only at the moment your heart stops," she replied. "But then you'll feel nothing at all."

"And then what?"

She shrugged, which was particularly unnerving without flesh. "Couldn't tell you. I'm not dead."

Orville squinted at her.

"I'm barely even death. This is a side gig."

"What if I don't play along?"

Popcorn growled like a submarine imploding. For once, Orville wished she wasn't smiling. The juxtaposition made him nauseated.

"You don't have to," she said softly. "Honestly, it won't even make it easier if you do."

"What are they paying you? I've got a little something under the mattress, if you catch my drift. I could make it worth your while to—"

"What, look the other way? You're the criminal, Orville. Not me."

"You're a murderer! Or you're about to be. Think about your immortal soul!"

"I'll tell you what. Answer one question for me, and I'll give you a head start."

"Let's hear it."

"What's my name?"

Tears welled in Orville's eyes. His hands began to tremble.

"You're scared," she said. "I understand. Just close your eyes. It's almost over."

"No!" Orville hugged himself and locked eyes on her, well, sockets. It was the last throes of a desperate man, clinging to life with everything he had.

"Shhh."

The wind howled high above the trees, but the breeze on the forest floor was barely strong enough to rustle the dead leaves. The shadows of the figures around the campfire stretched back into the proper darkness among the roots of the surrounding forest.

"Therein lies the essential conundrum of human nature," said the old man. He gathered his toga against the chill. "We possess so few instincts, and that is what separates us from the beasts."

"Let's talk about something else," said Jed.

"Survival," the old man went on, "preservation of the self. It's the one true instinct that we possess. It requires no thought."

"He knew what he was doing. And he's still there, skulking around on time he stole from me!"

"It's tragic, to be sure." The old man nodded. "But look at where you are now, eh? Not such a bad place to spend eternity."

Jed sighed up toward the treetops, watching the smoke from the fire curl skyward. Despite the rage thundering in his ears, he felt as though he'd sunk elbows-deep in warm tranquility. It reminded him of late summer nights around the campfires during apple picking season, when the sky stretched forever in every direction. But he hadn't sunk deep enough to forget, much less forgive.

"At least I got to watch him do it this time," said Jed, the firelight giving his eyes an even madder gleam than they'd had to begin with. "He won't do it again."

"Do tell," said the old man.

Jed found it off-putting, the way the old man hung on his every word. Jed had been a drifter in one life and a carrion bird in another. He'd been swatted away far more often than he'd been attended with any interest. Still, in the long dark of eternity, he supposed there wasn't much that didn't pass for entertainment.

"You know sharks?" asked Jed.

"I know of them." The old man grinned, clearly amused by his own wit. The long dark of eternity, indeed.

"They're what you call 'apex predators.' That means they're the top of the food chain. They've been around for millions of years, if you can believe it."

"There are stranger things under heaven." The old man cast a curious gaze upward. The sky was full of stars, and Jed got the impression the old man could read them in a way he couldn't.

"Yeah, I suppose. Anyhow, I reckon God felt bad for doing such a great job making sharks, so he built in a flaw. See, when a shark opens its mouth to gobble up a fish, it closes its eyes. Just for an instant. It ain't much, but if the fish is wily, I reckon he could use that second to zig while the shark zags and scamper off."

"And that's what your friend Orville did."

"He ain't my friend. Not for a long time now. He just proved it a second time."

"So he did." The old man nodded thoughtfully. "And you have your revenge."

"How do you figure?" Jed didn't attempt to soften his sneer of incredulity. When a man says something that dumb, it does him a disservice to let him indulge in the fantasy that he'd said something useful.

"Take heed," said the old man. He leaned in, locking eyes with Jed. "You are here despite the revenge you sought against your brother. You should count yourself fortunate you did not attain it."

"Fortunate." Jed ground his teeth.

"There is a place worse than this for the vengeful," warned the old man. "Worse yet for traitors. On its face, what happened to you was a tragedy twice over. But the torments that await Orville? Eternity is a very long time, and he's more than a traitor. He's unrepentant."

"He's a son of a bitch, that's what he is."

The old man shrugged. "Had he seized the opportunity to make amends, he might have earned himself a lesser torment. Some degree of absolution. Who knows? He can't run from death forever, but that's all he's got now."

"And it's better than he deserves!"

"Your life ended in the summer."

"It was January."

"Metaphorically speaking. Orville lived out the rest of the summer of his life, through the autumn, and into a very long winter. Death at his heels through unending winter. If that's not revenge, I don't know what is."

Jed was thankful for the silence that followed. Philosophers can be relied upon for the occasional contemplative silence, if nothing else. He watched the flames dancing in time with his own raging heart, and cursed Orville for a coward. He knew he should let it lie, but every breath that traitor drew was another dagger in Jed's back.

Lesser hells be damned. If reincarnation came around again, Jed hoped the weight of his soul was worth something with teeth.

THE TINKER'S SON

CASSONDRA WINDWALKER

The power of a Bane-Witch doesn't reside in a wand or a potion. The power of a Bane-Witch, like the power of a Boon-Witch, resides in her grimoire.

I hope you aren't making the same tired assumption so many people do, that Bane-Witches are inherently evil and Boon-Witches inherently good. It's a simple matter of balance. If justice is to mean anything, there must be curses to counter those who would squander and abuse their blessings. Although Bane-Witches and Boon-Witches tend to be fairly insular in their communities, it's more about scholarship and devotion than any aversion to the company of the other. There are at least a few festivals every year when they all come together, and even the occasional handfastings between the villages do occur.

As it happens, though, the tale you are reading is written in the grimoire of a Bane-Witch.

You've probably heard that no book will write itself, but that's precisely what I'm doing. I'll own it's a rare enough occurrence. Accomplishing a curse on herself is not something Bane-Witches are prone to do. Magic seems to be an inoculant to despair. And Margritte wasn't in despair. Her last act was one of love, not suicide. At least, that's what she thought. She probably fancied I'd be some sort of vessel for her soul, my pages a window through which she could still look out on her husband and remaining son. She believed when she poured her blood into my ink, her voice would script the words here. She didn't realize she was surrendering her life to give me my own.

I've known Margritte since she scrawled her first spell on my parchment at the age of four. Back then I was only a conduit: I received and passed on. The words she wrote when I became myself gave me back all those messages as memories. As if I had been merely sleeping all those years and had arisen at last.

Still, some of her pain lingers as my own, like the ghost-agonies of a dream whose edges mist away in the dawn light. As I bump along in the tinker's wagon on this bitterly cold morning, I cannot help but recall that other cold morning, the beginning of Margritte's end.

Bane-Witches. However benevolent their intent, even their gifts are curses. So now I possess life and longing and even love, but have no voice or arms with which to act. Only this endless scribbling on page after page. And what will become of me when the pages are full? I cannot tell, and still I cannot slow the pace of these words, any more than a mortal can cease their breathing and yet live. So I will put on Margritte as my dress to tell you this tale, pretend for these few minutes that I am more than this bundle of leather and parchment.

Winter's Turning. Not that anyone could tell, up high in the mountain wood, where even beneath the trees snow lay heaped in huge drifts that swallowed the boys whole as often as not. Margritte thought the happiest sound in the world had to be the high-pitched giggles and squeals of Peter and Jacques as they tumbled in and out of the white stuff. Their father had melted a clear path down to the valley village, but they would much rather disappear up to the tops of their knitted caps than take the easy route.

Still, even in the dark heights of the storm-topped mountain, Margritte imagined she could smell the jasmine promise of spring's return. The whole world celebrated this day, when Winter turned over the ash scepter to Spring and began his long dream. When morning broke, every day would grow a little longer, a little brighter, as Spring wielded her staff and began rousing the life sleeping in the frozen earth. Tonight, Margritte and her little family would feast together in the great stone hall of Goldgrym, and tomorrow they would join the village in festival, in dancing and spelling and songs. Bane-Witches would curse the padlocks of ice laid on the great river, and Boon-Witches would bless the somnolent salmon.

Witches were social creatures, who drew power and wisdom from the covens. But when Margritte had joined hands with a dragon-lord, she'd resigned herself to the relative solitude in which they lived. Unlike witches, the long-lived dragons thrived in space and silence. Handfastings between their races were rare. Witches possessed only the normal span of mortal years, while dragon-lords usually lived 600-700 years. Some might even be older. Every death of a dragon-lord ever recounted was a violent one: they were a martial species, so perhaps time was never an enemy of theirs, only the sword.

But Gregor had fallen for Margritte from the first time they met, when she was gathering mushrooms near his hall. Already ancient and strange and fierce, he knew he would have to watch her wither and die, knew he would have to watch their children and their grandchildren do the same, but he ached for every gray hair she would grow. Hungered to see time carve her face with its incautious fingers. Yearned to taste every inch of her skin, to recount to himself her secrets on dark nights after she had long left, to bury her sweet gold deep beneath his scales and feel its cut every time he flew.

This isn't a fairytale, after all. Dragon-lords cannot share their great age through a kiss or an exchange of blood. We all are what we are. And dragon-lords are the perpetual hoarders of all treasures and wisdom and the vagaries and foolishness of men. Gregor could only be Margritte's mate as a man. As dragon, he could carry her memory, build her library, add her stones to his towers, but he could grant her not a single extra day. And his children would be fully mortal, too—born only of the man, not the dragon.

Another Bane-Witch might have found her new existence, islanded on the mountain peak with the great quiet dragon, lonely, but not Margritte. She flourished there, like the tiny purple asters that peeped under every fern and bounded over the clinging moss. She buried herself in Gregor's massive library, learned old tongues mortals had long since forgot, became gardener and historian and astrologer.

Became mother, too. As a witch, all her schooling had been spent with other girls, so boys were such bizarre and mysterious creatures. She devoted herself to their taxonomy and fed all their wild impulses with more wild, more weird, more wonderful. But something went wrong. Or something had been wrong all along.

Perhaps some strain of the dragon did seep through their consummation. Perhaps Jacques' little heart beat too hard and fast for a mortal boy. Perhaps his breath blew like the winds of war that his father provoked with the great gusts of his wings. Perhaps he was simply stronger than he knew.

Winter's Turning. A day of delight, of rejoicing, of triumph over the darkness that every year seems so all-encompassing. On this Winter's Turning, though, something darker than the night rose in Jacques' heart and choked out that first trembling inhale of awakening spring.

Margritte and Gregor were never sure exactly what happened. Had Peter snatched a toy from his older brother? Had the four-year-old taunted the six-year-old, teased him into a rage with some small childish feud? Had a simple irritation flashed into an ungovernable fury?

They heard the howling. Jacques' voice, they instinctively knew, but inconceivably altered into something terrible and tragic, something too sorrowful to be dragon, too mad to be mortal.

Gregor had leaped from the window, taking his dragon form in a flash as he soared to answer his son's call. Margritte ran down the tower steps, caught in a nightmare in which every step came more slowly even as the distance lengthened. When at last she arrived in the forest clearing where violet-tinged smoke drifted in ominous warning, Gregor remained all drag-on, as if he had lost his man somewhere inside himself.

The trees around the clearing lay flat-out in a scorched circle. Gregor hunkered over something, his outstretched wings a fantastic gate of gold and silver and green. The air was filled with the sound of running water from the melted snow, inter-spersed with Jacques' undulating howls. Margritte searched for her husband in the dragon's bloodshot eyes, but all in the beast was fierce, feral, ungiving.

"Let me see," she pleaded, but he turned his great scaled back on her, drew whatever lay under his wings closer in.

Desperate to reach her children, she at last turned him to stone. It would have been an unforgivable act of betrayal, to use her art against him, but between them, as it turned out, nothing was unforgivable.

She crept forward, her boots squelching in the icy mud, bent nearly double beneath the stone wings to reach what lay at the dragon's feet. Her little Peter, barely recognizable but for the coat she'd sewn him of caribou hides Gregor brought her. His face, his head, was crushed, a mass of blood and swollen flesh. Beside him, curled in a tight spiral of despair and grief and self-loathing, lay Jacques, his howls reduced now to broken, hoarse-voiced growls of hopelessness.

Margritte fell to her knees in the cold sodden earth, her fingers scrabbling uselessly at her baby's limp shoulders, his shattered cheeks. Gregor was lost to the dragon because no man could bear this. No more could a mother. Margritte's womb emptied of all the pieces of her children she had kept, all the cells that made her mother, and became nothing but avenger, devourer, bane-bearer.

But first, she sobbed. Ugly, tearing, sobs that wrenched her stomach and left her throat raw. She sobbed until all her air sighed out of her in a long, exhausted exhale, and with it, all her mercy.

Jacques had struggled to his knees. His wiry little boy body shivered and sung like a fiddle string drawn too tightly. Desperately he hunched against his mother's side, his small, dirty, bloodstained hands clutching at hers. She could hear his voice, pleading, begging, asking for help no-one could give, but she pushed away the words.

Instead, she focused on her own.

As her spell left her lips, it took shape in the air. Jacques clung to her, his little bones pressing against her like a kitten pressing against its mother for protection from a cur, but irresistibly the incantation pulled him away. She stood beneath the stone wings of her husband, over the cooling body of her youngest son, while the dragon's heart beat a desperate and unheard appeal, and watched the hex settle over the skin of her oldest child.

His golden hair turned snow white, his skin a pallid, perfect gray. Every wound on little Peter's face found an outline on Jacques', scarlet lines of injury forever imbedded. His eyes, those warm hazel eyes she had loved so, were the last to fade. As she looked coldly into his ebbing gaze, she saw every shared silly laugh, every bedtime story, every drowsy unspoken avowal of love. She saw the milky-mouthed babe at her breast, the curious infant, the affectionate child. And then she saw the blue-eyed revenant, emptied of his soul, imbued only with his solitary and awful purpose.

He would be a collector of souls, a purveyor of justice. His duty would be to garnish those who had committed his own sin. What had once been Jacques would never grow, never age, never die. He would wander forever from damned to damned.

The cursed creature who looked so much like her son opened his mouth. Who knows what he would have said. If he would have pled, uselessly, still, for mercy. But Margritte raised her hand, and the boy fell silent. Those blue, blue eyes clung to hers a moment more, then he turned and trudged away, into the wood. Already the short day was ending, pale-faced stars looking down with grim silvered light.

Margritte gathered the broken remains of her dead child into her arms, rocked him close as she stumbled back to Goldgrym. She buried the little one beneath the stones of her husband's richest treasure hall. It took a long time, perhaps, but she had no thought of time. Every moment was an eternity, every eternity lost in the next hated breath. She measured the night in handfuls of dirt and the weight of stone.

The moon and the sun were rising together by the time she made her way back to the clearing. The mud and running water had turned to solid ice in the bitter cold. Margritte wrapped her fur cloak around her and sat down against the massive unmoving talons that stood fast still. Above her, beneath the stone scales, the dragon's heart beat slow and unstoppable, at once comfort and reproach.

They sat that way together, over the bloodstained ice, for days and nights and days again. At last, on a night with no moon, Margritte made her way to the clearing's edge and spoke the words that turned the stone to dust and set the dragon free.

Gregor shook out the great wings till they rang like bells then stood before his wife as a man. He raised his arms as if to pull her close but dropped them empty. His voice was low, graveled with agony.

"You have robbed us of both our sons."

Her answer came as barely a whisper.

"I am a Bane-Witch. I cannot allow evil to go unanswered. Not even evil innocent and unintentional. I must bring balance."

Margritte sensed a thousand arguments press against Gregor's lips, but he spoke none. What remained to be said? A

Bane-Witch's curse could not be undone.

"I am a father. I cannot allow him to walk alone."

Hot tears flooded Margritte's eyes, tears she thought long dry. They poured unchecked down her cheeks. "He must walk forever."

Gregor shrugged. "Who knows how long a dragon might live if only he would not fight? I will find him. Where he travels, I will travel with him."

"His task is grim."

"My heart is black enough to bear it."

Margritte's own blood felt thick with the hatred and rage, the adoration and adulation, of her husband. She struggled to breathe. Found just enough air.

"You know my days are short. I can only be an hour to your week. Will you carry my grimoire with you?"

Gregor's hand tightened into fists. She didn't know if he ached to hold her or to hit her. His eyes glistened like emeralds when he spoke.

"Bring me your book. I will carry it with me."

As she spun to hurry back to the hall, she heard him mutter fiercely, "Always."

Which brings the story back to me. When Margritte reached her own library, she hastily cast the spell that stole her life and granted mine. Gregor tired of waiting and came and found me there on my pedestal, Margritte's blood already absorbed in my thirsty pages. I don't know what became of her husk—her body seemed to simply fade out into the air. Perhaps some element of her even remains in that sad empty hall, bereft of all but its treasures and a tiny body buried under the stone.

I don't know Gregor like I knew Margritte, but even I experienced a thrill of terror at his towering grief when his fingers closed on my cover. I wondered how the castle did not fall.

He carried me with him down to the stables. Normally Margritte and the boys cared for the beasts; neither horses nor donkeys are much fond of dragons, whether they can see the scales or only sense them. But a handful of sugar and much soothing finally coaxed the stout little Panga to assent to the wagon. Gregor surprised me, taking his time loading the tin-roofed contraption with mattresses and gold and books, with food and wine and ale. I supposed he'd had time to make his plans while trapped in stone. I soon realized his new story would be that of a tinker and his son. Basic tools hung from the canvas walls of what was rapidly transforming from simple wagon to caravan.

It took us nearly two weeks of traveling to find Jacques. The sapphire-eyed revenant wasn't really Jacques, of course, but what else could we call him? And while he plainly experienced no real love or affection for Gregor, he assented to both the company and the deceit, playing the role of tinker's son as if it cost him nothing. And perhaps over time, the continual fellowship did transform into something close to comfort.

This new Jacques did not eat or drink, but sometimes he read the books Gregor had brought. When he'd read them all, Gregor would trade for new ones in the villages we passed through. In his soft, high-pitched little boy voice so uncannily familiar, Jacques would regale us with the horrors of the souls he harvested as he directed us to pause at this farmstead or that castle. He would unload his small wagon with its cheery little bell and ramble up, his welcome never questioned in spite of his eerie appearance. I don't know if that was some aspect of the magic, or just the weakness of the mortal mind for the figure of a child.

Soon enough he would return, his little tin teapot swinging from his fist or resting in the wagon bed. With every garnished soul, its patina grew darker.

Over the centuries, we settled into a sort of normalcy. Gregor no longer took his dragon form. I think he feared that as dragon, he would not resist his bellicose nature and might leave what remained of Jacques alone in the world. It did not seem to matter that Jacques was no longer a son; Gregor was still a father and could not be anything else. Perhaps some trace of kindness lingered in the ghoul, because he allowed Gregor to play the role without argument, consenting to the treatment of a child though by now he was hundreds of years old.

At night, Gregor slept on a narrow mattress in the caravan, or sometimes, when the air was hot, beneath the wheels where the starslung winds could gust unhindered over his skin. I wondered if he longed for the skies or if he had somehow killed that part of himself. Regardless, I was there, tucked up under his arm, against his chest, as he tossed and turned in restless dreams. I listened to his heart beat and thought of all the times Margritte had done the same, resting her head on the rise and fall of his breaths until all her existence became that steady pounding. I thought of her fingers curling through the hair on his chest, her nails tender knives against his skin, and wondered if Gregor thought of her, too, if he found in the weight of my pages the weight of that beloved head, if he imagined her breath sighing from my words to rest in his hands.

In all these centuries, he has taken no other wife. No friend has joined our ragged band. His is a loneliness complete. Fitting that the husband of a Bane-Witch would become a bane unto himself. He was the only one not cursed in the end, but that exception was its own hex, one he could not allow to stand. He has made shrift more devoutly than any penitent monk, and yet he will not forgive himself.

I do not know how he might explain Jacques to someone who spent more than a few minutes among us, anyway. These days, at least, his strange appearance is not so strange. Gregor is the odd one now. Some new pestilence has swept the world, a virus that leaves survivors scarred and marked by the ravages of the disease. It was highly contagious, infecting nearly everyone and killing many, but dragons are impervious to the illnesses of men. So Gregor's smooth skin is an aberration now, and Jacques' scarlet lines less so. Even his gray pallor is more easily accepted, put down to an unusual manifestation of the disease everyone knows too well.

Still, any who shared our journey would soon notice the child has no similarity with any other child on the earth. He never plays or cries, requires no food or drink or sleep. Aside from the stories of his collection, he is mostly silent. At night, while Gregor sleeps, he either lies wide-eyed in some unspoken communion with the stars or else walks soundlessly through long grass or dark trees, along river banks or bounded by the sea. He seems never restless, never lonely, never sad, never regretful. He only is.

We have come upon another Winter's Turning. You might think, after all these years, the bite of such an anniversary would have gone toothless, but it is not so. Gregor's countenance on this day is so dark, even I in my leather binding am inclined to shudder. His eyes recall the stone behind which he was imprisoned, and I swear I see dragon-fire flash beneath his skin. He always trades the traditional feast for fast, though I do not know if this is a deliberate act of contrition or simply an abhorrence of flesh on this day of all days.

For my part, I am consumed with thoughts of Margritte as winter and spring exchange their places. Her memories, her timbre beneath the spells, even the smell of her skin and hair, rise so powerfully within me I almost wonder if she is not truly caught somewhere in my glue still. I ache with a hollow womb I do not have. I weep dry tears for children lost I do not know. I thrill to the brush of Gregor's cold hands when he clutches me tight to his chest and stares at ghosts I do not see.

Jacques does not share the unease of the calendar. He notes Gregor's condition with his hard blue gaze and does not remark on it. For him, it is only another day among uncountable days.

No snow this year. I want to believe that will make it easier for Gregor, some disconnect between the feast-day of the past and the present. And this world is so different from the one where our story began. Most of what remains of the world's population is hunched in cities, living, dying, working, eating, sleeping in shifts intended to limit their exposure to one another. Society has become a strange machine intent only on its own survival as a machine, all its persons reduced to cogs and wheels and gears with their precise duties to perform. Those who live in the countryside still are less altered, more easily able to avoid new infection without drastic measures.

New gods have risen, and the Bane-Witches and Boon-Witches have vanished entirely or retreated into hiding. But some magic cannot be denied. This new society has given Winter's Turning a new name, but they celebrate the Solstice much the same. Instead of bonfires, the cities are strung with lights. Feasts and dances and gift-exchanges mark the celebration of day's return.

Here, in the south of the continent, the frigid air is wretched with rain instead of the snow of Gregor's beloved mountains. Our caravan now is a tiny wooden house built on the back of an old pickup bed, all the Pangas long since dead. We rumble slowly through the city streets, the insistent cheer of all the many-colored lit windows a painful contrast to the unrelenting gray grief of the mourning sky. I lie on the bench seat between a hard-jawed Gregor and an incurious Jacques. As always, we follow his direction, turning when he says turn, driving till he says stop.

Soon enough we leave the city behind, just as the bells ring out the changing of the shifts. We pass those waiting to enter the city where raincoat-clad guards stand with thermometers, checking each of the travelers for any sign of infection. Though almost all the population who survived the first wave of the virus are immune to its return, it has proven unusually wily in its adaptation and mutation, and new, deadlier strains continue to cast out their long tendrils. Perhaps the virus will scour the earth clean of these mortals eventually, and the dragon-lords will return to the skies. If any of them but Gregor even remain. They were so few in number to begin with, and rather prone to death in battle. We have not met another in our travels for at least three hundred years now.

We are well out of town when Jacques rouses. He points to an old farmhouse standing alone in the pouring rain, and we turn onto the long drive without question. Gregor parks the pickup under a copse of weeping trees and shuts off the engine.

Jacques jumps down and goes to the back to unload his wagon. He trudges through the cold rain in his small boots as if he cannot feel the icy cold, a cap obscuring the snow-white hair so he might appear to be only a tow-headed blond. I hear the little red bell ringing merrily beneath the roar of the rain and the gusts of the wind and wonder if the soul inside those doors knows it is being summoned by that call.

Jacques clambers up the wooden steps with the tin teapot clutched in his hand and knocks on the door. A willowy young woman with long black hair opens the door and stares down at the child in surprise.

She lets him in, of course. They always do.

Perhaps only a few minutes later, or perhaps hours, I shake myself from drowsiness as the chiming of the bell marks his return. He puts his wagon away and climbs up beside me, a gentle warmth emanating from the teapot on his lap.

Gregor starts the truck, and we pull away from the farmhouse. Jacques leans back against the seat and closes his eyes. I have never known if he is truly tired, if the act of gathering these souls draws some of his own eternal energy, or if he has merely learned the subterfuge. His childish tones begin the tale of his latest acquisition, and my ink flows across an empty page.

Stefana inhaled deeply, drawing the fragrance of cinnamon and oranges into her lungs as if it might carry the peace of the season into her trembling belly. Festive music poured from her small speakers, and every corner of the room was festooned with lights. The table, garnished with pine boughs, and set with red-ribboned china, invited all to sit and be filled. Platters of cheeses and sweets and yeasty breads covered the thick oak, and glasses brimming with red wine perched at the edge of every empty plate.

She wasn't sure why she'd felt compelled to put on such a feast. Outside, rain pounded against the windows so that she could hardly see even a few feet into the yard. Moated by cold and solitude, she drew her sweater more tightly across her shoulders and sank into the old wooden rocking chair, staring at the empty chairs surrounding the set table.

This was the first Solstice without Mama and Raquel. Papa had been the first to die, shortly before the last Solstice. He'd fallen ill while delivering produce to the city. No visitors were allowed in hospitals: too much chance of contracting the disease themselves and then continuing to spread it to the community outside. They'd called him several times a day, but every day the calls grew shorter and more difficult as his lungs labored to hold air. Then came the day a nurse answered the phone and explained how Papa had been intubated and could no longer speak. Sometimes, if the nurses weren't too busy, they would hold the phone to Papa's ear for a while and let them talk to him, at least, even if he couldn't answer. Raquel and Stefana wondered privately if Papa were even truly conscious, or if the nurses only offered a compassionate fiction to his wife, but they shared their doubts only with each other, never with Mama.

Then came the night when the phone rang in their house instead of in Papa's room, and he was gone. There could be no funeral; aside from the transport of food and supplies and such necessaries, the city was shut down. Even burials were an unaffordable luxury; crematoriums smoked day and night. Postal service had been severely restricted, so ashes were scattered in the rivers and canals of the city, an awful anonymity as ubiquitous as death itself.

Neighbors left notes and letters and drooping flowers on their doorstep. If Papa had died just a few weeks earlier, people would have brought casserole dishes and baked goods, but already the virus had stolen such impulses. Who knew what infection lingered on a dish, and who dared return one? Along the fence that marked the beginning of the drive, friends tied bright-colored ribbons, a silent tribute to Papa's life.

Raquel, two years older than Stefana, was subsumed by grief. Every night, she tortured herself with replaying their father's final lonely days. Stefana would climb into her bed and rock her sister in her arms while she wept, frightening, convulsive sobs so strong Stefana feared her heart might burst from the pain. The sterile hospital room, empty even of nurses aside from the most urgent of tasks, the sounds of the respirator as it forced air into Papa's mucus-filled lungs, the intrusion of tubes and needles, the indignity of dying only as a punctured husk under a sheet.

"Did he know?" she begged Stefana, a hundred times. "Did he know we loved him? Did he know we were here, thinking of him, every minute? Did he think we had abandoned him? Did he know?"

Stefana, her own eyes blind with tears, stroked her sister's sweaty hair and promised her he knew, he had to know. But she felt she lied, and Raquel felt it, too. How could they ever be forgiven? It didn't matter that there'd been no way to break into the hospital, to sit by his side until his heart finally failed. What was possible was irrelevant. All that mattered was loss, and the loss was complete.

When Papa died, something broke in Mama. Somehow she kept the grief at bay, permitted it no entry. Stefana understood that better than Raquel's awful darkness. Stefana found herself more moved by her sister's sadness than by her father's death. Was he even dead? She could hardly force her mind to believe it. He had been so strong and healthy when he left that morning.

He'd refused to take the girls this time, but only out of what he described as an "abundance of caution." He'd thrown a face mask onto the seat of the truck for when he reached the city, and Mama had stuck a bottle of hand sanitizer in his pocket, but they'd been convinced they were being far more careful than was actually necessary. Stefana kept picturing him as he'd been that late autumn morning, his dark face ruddy with cheer as he waved a final farewell out the open window before turning onto the road. It was too surreal to accept that was the last time she'd ever see him. To not say goodbye, even to the dead, to be robbed of the mercy of a funeral, made it impossible for her heart to accept he was truly gone. Every time she heard an engine on the road, she looked out the window, expecting still to see his truck pulling into the drive.

That surreality was where they lost Mama. Stefana knew Papa was dead, however little she could conceive of it. But Mama found a way out. She simply refused it. Without a body, without a farewell or a grave to visit, Mama chose instead to wait. Papa would return, she said. She stopped cooking and cleaning, stopped putting up preserves or managing the books. She spent her days sitting on the front porch swing, watching the road, her nights on the couch.

At first, the girls left her to her fantasy. Perhaps, they told each other, she needed the space and time to accept the truth. Perhaps this was a normal aspect of the denial phase of grief. They would brush her hair for her as she sat in the porch swing, persuade her to let them help her change her clothes every couple of days. The coaxed her to eat and drink just enough to keep her alive.

Stefana did her best to keep the farm going. She tried to keep her mind occupied by poring over the seed catalogues and reading articles on organic farming and planning the next spring's rotation of crops. Anything to keep the unyielding despair of the household at bay.

Meanwhile, their private isolation mirrored the marooning suffered by the whole world. As the virus continued to race unchecked through city after city, people everywhere retreated into solitude. Trips even to the village were rarely undertaken and then only with extreme caution. All commerce was handled remotely, and people avoided each other fastidiously on the street. The scars that marked a survivor became a sort of currency of consolation. Disfigurement meant you were safe. You had survived and no longer posed any risk of being a carrier. People began segregating themselves by their scars.

It didn't seem to matter that the recovered couldn't get sick again. Within a few months, when the virus would begin to mutate, that would no longer be true, but already people had learned to substitute icon for faith. Skin color, religion, gender no longer stratified society, but the scars did. Few things provoked more horror or distrust than a face unmarked by illness. Survivors moved freely and wielded all power among those who remained. The uninfected huddled more alone than ever and waited for sickness and death to reach them.

Stefana and Raquel and their mother were such an islanded household, though more out of the madness that had overtaken them than fear. Mama and simple survival required all their energy. Even if they had been tempted to risk unnecessary excursions, they hadn't the will. Every day Mama slipped further and further away, drifting toward a horizon they couldn't see.

At last Raquel persuaded Stefana they had to make Mama see, had to make her accept that Papa was dead and wouldn't be coming back. Cocooned in her own less-fervent denial, Stefana had been reluctant to force Mama into a grief so terrible, but even she grew frightened of Mama's utter surrender to her hopeless wait.

Even so, they didn't think they were making any headway until one cold spring morning when they woke to find Mama gone. The front door stood open, an icy drizzle dampening the threshold. Muddy boot prints led down the drive.

The girls searched the farm, calling her name, but found

no sign of her. Stefana was gathering face masks and gloves so they could venture out in the car to look for her when a vehicle pulled into the drive and stopped by the fence.

A man Stefana recognized from the village but whose name she didn't know stepped out and walked around to the passenger door. Stefana and Raquel stood on the porch, straining anxiously to see in the pale gray light. The man helped Mama, wrapped in a thick blanket, her hair soaking wet and slicked to her head, out of the car. He gave her a little push, and Mama began trudging slack-faced toward the house.

The man waved at the sisters before getting back into his car and pulling away. "I found her in the river!" he shouted between cupped hands.

Raquel gasped and started as if she would leap off the porch and run to meet her mother, but Stefana seized her arm in an iron grip. "No," she hissed. "No. Did you see his face? Smooth-skinned. Mama might be infected."

Raquel stared at her in horror. "We can't leave her out here."

"Of course not. We can put her in the shed."

"Have you lost your mind?"

"Have you?" Stefana gave her a shake. "You know what can happen. Come with me. We'll get blankets and pillows, drag a space heater out there with an extension cord. We'll bring her food and water and clean clothes. It'll just be a couple weeks. Just till we know she's safe."

Raquel glanced back at her mother, slowly placing one foot in front of another. Tears, always ready these days, ran down her cheeks. "Stefana," she pleaded.

"It's the only way. If you help me, we can get it ready faster and she won't have to stand out here so long."

Reluctantly Raquel nodded. Stefana pushed her toward the door and yelled to her mother, "Wait there, Mama. We're going to get things ready for you."

Mama stopped instantly, without raising her gaze from the ground. An eerie horror suffused Stefana. She shook off the sensation and rushed to help her sister transform the shed into a living space.

They worked as quickly as they could, but even so, Mama was shivering violently by the time they returned and directed her to the shed. Stefana turned on the kettle to make a hot cup of tea and a bowl of soup. Raquel huddled under an umbrella outside the shed door, speaking to their mother through the thin walls. Stefana had to practically drag her back in the house when she left the soup and tea on a tray at the doorstep.

"What did she say?" Stefana asked Raquel once they were both back inside.

Raquel struggled against a sob, shaking her head. "She believed us. She finally believed us. But she said if Papa is in the river, that's where she wants to be too. I don't think she understands he's dead. That she'll be dead, too, if she joins him that way. She's—she's like a child. Confused."

Exhaustion fell over Stefana, and she staggered beneath its weight. "What can we do?"

Raquel walked over to the window. "She took the soup and tea, at least. I'll put a padlock on the door. So she can't slip out and go back to the river. Maybe she just needs more time. She'll get better. She has to."

Three days later, Stefana heard Mama coughing when she took her breakfast.

"It could just be a cold," Raquel argued. "Or pneumonia. She was in that cold water. There's no reason to think it's the virus. We need to bring her in where we can take better care of her."

"No." Stefana was adamant. "We can give her everything she needs, but she has to stay in the shed. We can't risk it. You know if she's sick, we'll both catch it. There'll be no-one left to take care of her. Then what will become of her? We'll take medicine out there. Extra blankets."

Raquel turned away from her sister, her silence a condemnation in itself. But Stefana knew she was right. And two days later, when the lesions appeared on Mama's skin, Raquel couldn't deny the virus had found them at last.

But the knowledge only fired her determination to bring Mama inside.

"Papa died alone," she said. "There was nothing we could do. But Mama is right there." She pointed at the shed. Stefana followed her finger. In the incongruous cheer of spring sunlight, the shed looked like a fairytale cottage rather than a death house. But Stefana was undeceived.

"What do you think we can do? They won't let us in the city with her in this condition. And even if we could somehow get her to a hospital, we'd have to leave her there alone. It's not as if we can help her breathe better because she's in a bed in the house instead of on that cot out there. We'll just die alongside her."

"We could save her," Raquel insisted. "She's delirious out there. We can keep her propped up in her own bed, make sure she takes her medicine, get something hot down her throat. She has a chance with us. And we're both young. Strong. Maybe we won't get it. Maybe we'll fight it off if we do. But she is for sure going to die out there if we leave her alone."

Stefana gritted her teeth before forcing herself to speak slowly. "Mama doesn't even want to survive. She wants to die. She wants to be with Papa. How is it a mercy to force her to live just long enough to kill her own children with her infection? She went after this. We can't save her from herself."

Raquel opened her mouth then snapped it shut. She went upstairs, slamming her bedroom door behind her. Stefana shook her head wearily and retreated to her own room.

She wasn't sure what roused her a few hours later, but she moved to the window to look out at the shed as she now did a hundred times a day. Dread pooled sickeningly in her belly when she saw the door standing open in the pale moonlight.

She ran downstairs and threw open the back door. Raquel was struggling across the backyard, half-holding, half-carrying her mother's limp body. She paused, panting, and raised her head to meet Stefana's horrified gaze.

"Raquel, no! How could you do this?"

"My mother is not going to die alone." Raquel spoke flatly. "Just get out of the way. I'll take care of her myself."

Terror, mad and noisy, roared in Stefana's ears so loudly she could hear nothing else. She disappeared from the doorway only long enough to grab the shotgun. The sound of the barrel pumping barely registered.

"Stop, Raquel. Go back to the shed."

Raquel only laughed, a short huff of disbelief. "Hide in your room, Stefana," she replied. "We're coming in."

Pulling the trigger was shockingly easy, a bare breath of movement, a caress of the finger. Raquel hardly had time to look startled as she dropped, her mother's weight falling across her bloody chest.

Choking back a sob, Stefana pumped the shotgun again, sent a second bullet into her mother's prone form. She couldn't leave her lying there to suffer in the yard. She couldn't drag her back into the shed without infecting herself. It was the only merciful thing to do.

The bodies took much longer to decompose, even fully exposed to the elements, than Stefana had anticipated. For weeks the overwhelming rancid sweet odor filled the house, and the backyard swarmed with death eaters of every sort. Every breath she took, she imagined she inhaled the rotting flesh of her mother and sister. Day by day, the accusing stares became more macabre, more ghoulish, and still she could not resist losing herself in those eyeless gazes even long after the ravens had plucked their sockets clean.

She intended to wait until little was left but bones and then bury them together, but an unspeakable dread of the corpses took stronger hold of her every day. She would stand at the windows and watch the scavengers feast, unable to look away, unable to invade that space now sacred. She locked the back door and kept the windows closed. The heaped carcasses became a holy relic whose sacred ground she dared not sully with her bloody feet.

When the Solstice turned, she cooked a feast fit for a dozen and set the table for four. Mama and Raquel would surely join her tonight, at least. She'd strained her ears listening for their voices, for a familiar footfall on the stairs. She longed after ghosts, but not even her guilt haunted her. But everyone knew the oldest magic was at work on Solstice. Tonight they would be together. Tonight they would celebrate the turn.

So when she heard the tinny tinkling of a bell coming up the front walk, her heart leapt into her throat. Papa! Had Papa come home too? At last they would be reunited. She'd rushed to the door, too certain of her hope to even look out the window.

She'd been stunned to find a young child standing there, a pale-faced little boy whose scarlet scars proclaimed him safe. A strange pickup truck with a little wooden house built into its bed was parked on the drive. A tinker, she realized, an endangered occupation in these times. Who would send a child to knock on a strange door on Solstice Night, with nothing but a teapot in his hand?

Jacques' voice fades into the night, lost in the rumble of the tires over the dirt road. He never tells the end. I wonder if the souls he gathers are relieved to be rid of the weight of their lives at last, if guilt and grief make surrender easy, or if they suffer the same terror and anguish they inflicted on others. Jacques doesn't say.

The truck jars over a pothole, and the little wagon bell rings faintly from the caravan. Beside me, Gregor flinches ever so slightly. He keeps his eyes on the moonlit road ahead as if he fears to look at the creature that wears his son's skin. I wonder who he misses more—the broken baby Peter, the Bane-Witch, or the son to whose wraith he has sworn such unswerving and terrible allegiance. Perhaps most he misses the sky.

FROSTBITE

DALENA STORM

Y*ou might as well be dead.*
        This is what I repeat to myself over and over as I storm out of the common room and down the stairs and out the front door, not even bothering to go upstairs first and grab my coat.

You might as well be dead, Kay. You're never going to amount to anything. You humiliated yourself again. What if you can't pretend to be happy anymore? What if you can't keep convincing yourself that everything is okay? If you can't do that, well then fuck you, you might as well go kill yourself.

It's fucking freezing outside—snowing again—and I know I should turn around and go back upstairs. If I want to throw this fit then I should at least take my coat.

Don't be stupid, Kay. You just don't think!

That's my mom talking. She lives in my head, too. She's always there: criticizing me. It's not enough for everyone *else* to criticize me; not enough for *me* to do it; *she* has to do it.

I wouldn't have to, Kay, if you'd just think *for once!*

"Oh, go to Hell, Mom!"

I am hardly aware of myself yelling this out loud to the night sky. But other people are aware of it: they stop and stare at me—hey, who's that? Oh, it's just c-r-a-z-y Kay, out without her coat again. *Where did she come from?* I can feel them thinking. *Why does she dress like that? Doesn't she know it's below freezing outside?*

I would tell them to go and go to Hell too, but I'm not brave enough to do that so I just bite my tongue and run away with my tail between my legs like a coward, because I am a coward—too chicken to do anything worthwhile, too chicken to even kill myself.

This campus is fucking beautiful. That's another thing that kills me. It's not the world *I* came from; not the world belong to. And this is obvious to everyone—not just to me. I stand out like a sore thumb. I am a blemish on all this beauty. I am awkward—worse than awkward—I am *poor*, God forbid! Poor! On this campus? In this country? You might as well be ...

I don't even know where I'm going. I'm just walking as fast as I can. I just want to get away from all the people, all the judgment, all the thoughts. Anyone who tells you that mind reading is impossible is clearly full of shit because I always know what people are thinking. I feel every little judgmental thought they ever throw my way, because I am like hyper-attuned to that shit. My mom taught me all about it. I know all the signs. *Did you just hear what she said? Why is she dressed like that? Why is she so quiet? Is she okay?*

"Are you okay?"

I ignore the person who said just this and hurry on past them. What does it matter if I'm okay? What if I'm *not* okay—is *that* okay? Because the answer is no—it is obviously not okay to be not okay. That's like a tautological definition. And so, why answer when the answer is going to be the wrong one? That's why I don't talk in class. I know my answers are all wrong, but they're the only ones I have. Sometimes I want to share them so bad I feel like screaming, but I can't just start screaming in class because that would be effing crazy. Then they'd expel me for sure. I'm hanging on by a thread as it is. And it is *so* not okay to be the amount of "not okay" that I am that there is no way I can ever tell anyone. I just have to keep it hidden and buried deep inside and hope it somehow goes away all on its own.

I bury my hands deep in my pockets, searching for warmth against my skin. Not that there's much of it to be had, considering how skinny I've gotten lately. That's intentional, by the way. Don't ever let anyone tell you that you can't control your body. You can control *whatever the hell you want*. Even your life. Even your death.

The snow is falling thick and fast and I'm shivering uncontrollably. It makes me want to laugh. It hurts, and the sad thing is I don't want it to hurt. Something soft in me recoils from it but as soon as I sense that softness *I want to effing kill myself* and this urge is even stronger than the soft part that wants to shy away from the pain. So this mad raving lunatic RAGE deep inside carries me to the very edge of campus and then up this hill behind the art museum that my boyfriend took me up once back when I thought maybe someone could love me. He almost did but then he didn't. It's not like I blame him because honestly if I'd been dating me then I would have had to leave my crazy ass, too.

Hiking up the hill leaves me breathless and warms me some. The tears on my face are freezing against my skin.

What are you doing, Kay? says a little voice deep inside of me, but it's only a quiet little voice—so quiet I ignore it, because no one ever wants to listen to anyone who's quiet. *Just give it up, Kay. You might as well.*

So here is another point at which I should turn back. I have climbed up the hill. Here is the forest. There are the trees, covering darkness. It's a full moon out: just my luck. They say full moons make people go crazy. But what if you're crazy already? Does it undo it? That would be nice.

The snow is falling lighter now. Behind me is the campus, where everything is warm. I could go back to my dorm, where the other students might be done laughing now. Maybe one of them even feels bad about how they acted—maybe even regrets it just a bit, realizing I wasn't joking, I was deadly serious.

Or even if I don't go back and see them, I could go back to my room and curl up in my bed. I could warm my freezing limbs and cry into my pillow like I always do, and then tomorrow the campus shuttle would come and take me to the airport and I'd have to go home.

Christmas at home.

The thought fills me with nausea that makes my decision easy. Forward it is.

When my ex took me up here, we stopped at this hill. He made a fire because he thought it would impress me. It totally did. I fell in love with him instantly—big mistake in retrospect. Never fall in love with someone who won't love you back in equal measure. This is something I'm still learning. It's like I'm hardwired to fail at it.

Point being, I have no idea how deep these woods are or where they go. I am getting so cold I know it's becoming dangerous. I'm not stupid, in spite of the fact that I'm quiet, in spite of what my mom likes to say in my head. I know when I'm getting into trouble, and when I do it *anyway*, it's not out of stupidity. It's out of hatred.

I know it's a problem to hate yourself or whatever, but the problem is I don't know how to stop doing it.

I am choking out sobs as I wander through the forest, imagining talking to my imaginary therapist. Does this make me crazy? My therapist laughs. *So long as you're asking if you're crazy, you're not crazy.* But I'm talking to you in my head. You're not even real. *What is reality?* My therapist lifts her pen to her lips like this was a very intelligent question to ask. She thinks I should ponder on it for a while, so I do, tromping through the snow, kicking it with my boots that I ordered from Amazon when I found them on discount. They're too tight and they hurt my toes but it's because my feet are too wide, so really my feet deserve it for being the wrong damn size.

What is reality?

I open and close my fingers, making fists. I raise them to my lips and blow on them. They hurt. A lot. I'm going to get frostbite. I know this just like I know when the dining hall is serving bacon because I smell it when I'm on the stairs. If I don't turn back now, I'm going to get frostbite.

My mom, for once, is silent on the matter. I was expecting something snarky, but she's decided to pipe down. This relieves me somewhat. Perhaps I was right to come out here. Perhaps this is my destiny—what will happen if I push forward and go through with it?

Let's find out.

This is a different kind of voice. This one is female, too, but mischievous. I'm pretty sure I like her. She might be like a fairy. She might make something really good happen out here, something I'm not expecting. That would be neat.

"Okay," I say out loud, because I'm alone out here so it doesn't matter if I talk or not. It feels nice to make my thoughts known, to express what I'm thinking. I decide to keep going with it. "I think I might end up dying out here tonight, but honestly that might be better than going home, so I might be okay with it."

Snot is dripping down my upper lip and I wipe it away with my dead-numb fingers. They've almost reached the stage where they don't hurt anymore. That's when you're supposed to really start worrying.

With my arms wrapped in front of me I start trotting through the forest, trying to get my shivering under control, but this is obviously a lost battle—lost from the moment I left without my coat. I am wearing a hoodie, but this is quite insufficient. What will they think when they find me out here tomorrow? *Will* anyone find me? Or will they not even notice I'm gone?

The thought strikes me no one is going to notice I'm missing for quite a while. No one is going to check on me. No one will make sure I've boarded my flight. My ex has moved on and is happily with another girl, one who is *much fatter* than me, so at least I can hate her for that. I have to hate her for something, because if I don't, it'll mean she's better than me. Which will mean I'm worthless—my greatest fear.

To distract myself from this thought, I start to sing a song. "Over the field and through the woods, to grandmother's house we go!" except my lips are numb so the "v"s and "f"s come out more like "b"s which makes me sound completely ridiculous. That makes me laugh and that's when I realize I've come as far as I can go.

I don't know where I am. I'm deep in the woods. I sink down with my back against the trunk of a tree and wrap my arms around myself and shiver and wait for death.

This wasn't how I wanted to go. I wanted to be old and married and in bed, with my arms around the other person so that we could go at the same time and neither of us would be left alone.

The thought of the kind of death that I want and I'm not getting makes me cry. I double over, weeping. I wish someone would find me now. I wish someone would find me now and fall in love with me and save me. I wish someone would love me enough to save me from myself.

Of course, that isn't going to happen. I'm going to freeze to death instead.

This is so pitiful I think even my mom would feel bad for me. Even my mom would say, "Kay, it's okay now, please come back inside."

But it's too late for that now, Mom. I'm already out here! I don't know how to get back. I'm sorry. It's too late.

A sudden beam of light cuts through the darkness, nearly startling me out of my skin. I let out a yelp because who the hell is out here at this hour and what if they're a serial killer?

Of course, it might seem ironic to be afraid of a serial killer when you were just baiting death. But some deaths are better than others, and a death where I'm in some degree of control is far preferable to a death in which someone else is.

"Hello?" comes a voice. It's a female voice, but the affect isn't normal. It makes me feel afraid. It's a voice with a threat in it. The dark figure approaches, closer and closer, footsteps crunching in the snow, and I realize this is it. Human, banshee, demon—whoever she is, she's got me now, and it's all my fault. I deserve my punishment. I close my eyes and start to pray. *I take it back, I take it back*, I think to the imaginary being in the heavens who maybe has some power I honestly don't know. But the imaginary being doesn't care to listen to me, perhaps because I'm a heathen mostly non-believer, and so the light from the flashlight comes swinging through the trees and lands right on my face so that I don't dare to open my eyes. I am exposed, visible. I want to disappear.

"Oh my God, are you okay?"

The voice sounds normal now. But—is it a trick? If I open my eyes, what will I find in front of me? My mind conjures up horrible images. I become aware of my own breathing. No one is moving, no one is talking. The light is still on my face.

I lift up a hand to shade my eyes and then I peer up into the brightness, blinking. A shadowy form materializes above me in the darkness behind the flashlight. Given what I can see, I'd say there's a fifty-percent chance the figure might be a normal human. I decide to take that bet. Okay, Kay. Time to talk. This woman asked you a question, didn't she?

"Uh, yeah," I sniffle, and wipe my nose and eyes with the back of my sleeve. "I was just out for a walk."

My voice sounds funny, like the voice of a total, emotionally-wrecked, discombobulated liar. Discombobulated is a funny word. I bet I couldn't say it now with my totally numb lips.

I struggle to my feet, trying to make it look natural, but my limbs aren't cooperating or responding like they normally do.

"Yeah. Me too," says the woman, who seems to have taken my totally false statement at face value. Unless she's a demon trying to deceive me. I peer through the darkness, unable to make out what she looks like. "I'm getting kind of cold, though," she says in her convincing simulation of a normal human voice. "Think I might head back."

"Oh … kay?" I can't quite follow what's going on here. This isn't what a normal human would do in these circumstances. A normal human would notice I've been sitting here freezing to death and they'd phone 9-1-1 and try to help me out. But a demon would be smart enough to know that a human would act that way, so … could she be neither? Not a human or a monster?

"Nice to meet you," she says, and then she *turns the other way*.

Her flashlight illuminates the path in front of her and I see that somehow, I have stumbled on to a genuine path through the forest, where the trees have been cleared and the way ahead is even. She takes a step, and then another, and I realize she's not kidding.

She found me, but now it's up to me to follow her.

Damn, that is clever. Now whatever I do, it's all my own fault. Isn't that how God expelled Adam and Eve from the garden of Eden? Rather than just kicking them out on the up-and-up, he gave them an apple tree and said, "Don't ever try to think for yourself." So what were they supposed to do? Eden was already spoiled by the presence of something off-limits. Whether they listened or didn't listen, the effect was essentially the same. Living for eternity in blissful ignorance has never been my idea of paradise. If you offer me an apple, I am going to damn well eat it.

So I get up off my ass and I follow her retreating form. Lead the way, oh dark savior, lead me to the depths of despair—to anywhere but here. Whatever torment you have for me, I might as well face it. It's better than staying put and never knowing what's out there.

The longer I walk after her without saying anything the more scared I feel, like I'm Eurydice following Orpheus, but she doesn't know I'm here and that not-knowing is what's going to be my downfall. I feel like a stalker, a wraith, a hanger-on, a ghost. It strikes me that I could already be dead and just not know it. What if no one ever notices me again? What if I'm condemned to fully become the part of myself I hate—the part that quietly, invisibly haunts the life that it longs for?

Finally, I can't take the silence any longer. I have to break it, no matter what happens. I give a little cough.

The figure in front of me nearly jumps out of her skin and shrieks. The flashlight swings back around so it's shining in my eyes.

"Hey," I say, giving a big smile into the brightness so I don't look too frightening. It's just me—little ol' Kay. Nothing scary here. Just a normal girl. "Uh … I think I'm lost," I say, trying to appeal to the humanity of this creature.

"You scared the *crap* out of me," she cries, sounding very much like a human woman, and it has the effect on me it always has when human women react to me like this. A long snake of humiliation coils itself up in my belly, and I remember my earlier chant. It is very hard to make myself keep going toward her, to not turn around and run screaming back into the woods.

"Sorry," I manage to say nevertheless, digging my finger-nails into my palms as hard as I can in the hope that a little bit of pain will give me strength. Unfortunately, I'm too numb. I can't feel a thing.

"You're lost? Jesus! Why didn't you say something?"

I have no answer for this question. I never do. So I just shrug and slap a doofus-y smile on my face. Let her decide to take pity on me, the poor lost imbecile. It's what a normal person would do. If she's a smart demon-woman, she'll figure that out.

"Well … come on," she says with a sigh. "You can come home with me, I guess."

The warmth that leaks out of my heart has an instant effect on my body. Despite her half-hearted acquiescence, I can feel a chemical reaction happening. She took pity on me. She didn't hate me, didn't laugh. I'll do anything now to make her love me; I'll lick the dirt from her demonic boots if that's what she wants.

Come on, Kay, don't be dumb! Don't fall in love with her already!

But it's too late. Come on—Florence Nightingale effect? When someone saves you from certain death are you going to *not* fall in love with them?

But I try as hard as I can to fight it. *She doesn't want you to love her. What if she knew what you were thinking right now? She'd be horrified. She'd leave you back there in the snow. Just focus on something else. Be* normal *for once, for Christ's sake!*

"So, do you live out here?" I manage to say. My voice makes me sound like a total creep, like a stalker who was just waiting in the woods for her to come along so I could *latch* onto her.

"What? Yeah. I mean no. I mean—sorry." She laughs. "I'm a little distracted."

"Oh. No worries."

I fall in step next to her. *She's* a little distracted. *She's* not paying attention. This is great, because it means she's missed out on all my weirdness, and I can have a fresh start. Okay, Kay. Let's do this.

"It's so cold out," she says.

"Yeah," I say through chattering teeth. We are really paling around now, sharing an experience.

"Full moon out, too."

"Yeah," I say, searching desperately for something else to add to the conversation. I've never been good at small talk. Plus, now that I'm moving again, I can feel everything isn't as it should be, and the state of my poor body is distracting me. Which is worse, I wonder? My fingers or my toes? My ears or my nose?

The walk back to her house is both exhilarating and mind-numbing. I alternate between elation and despair, excitement and dread. Now that we're walking side-by-side it seems clear she's not a demon. But if she *wanted* to be, I mean if she *wanted* to do something demonic or whatever, all I'm saying is, I'd let her.

"So," she says, when we get to a little cabin-in-the-woods-y type place, "here we are. My folks' summer home. Don't worry.

They're not here now."

"You're not a student?" I say, surprised despite myself.

"A student?" she looks at me in the dark night. Then she laughs. "I guess you can't see very well out here. No. But thanks."

Once we're inside with the lights on I can see she's not as young as I thought she was, not as young as she sounds, but it's not like she's old, she's a *good age*, an age when people stop being so full of themselves and get a little bit of wisdom and a little bit of experience. Probably it's the age I am deep in my heart, not that anyone would know it because no one knows me that well.

This woman—who is even more beautiful than I might have imagined or hoped for—rubs her face and then looks at me and apologizes again.

"I'm sorry for being so rude. This just isn't a good night for me."

"You're not being rude."

"I'm not? Oh. Good. Well, anyway. Come on in. Sit down. My name's Alice. What's your name? I should have asked you earlier. Do you want some coffee?"

"I'm … Kay," I say, but then I can't figure out how to answer the second question. Coffee or no coffee? It's not like it's hard. Just a yes or no question. Come on, Kay! Just pick one!

She looks at the expression on my face and for some reason she laughs.

"Of course you don't want coffee. Who wants coffee on a night like this? Tequila. That's just what the doctor ordered. Am I right or am I right?"

This is an easier sort of question—only one option to choose from. I nod my affirmation, relieved not to have to make a decision. I am afraid that any second now she is going to fall into some normal pattern of behavior and ask me what I was really doing out there. Then she'll send me packing back off into the night, which is the last place I want to go. I don't trust myself out there. I can feel I was getting into a dangerous place, a place I very nearly didn't return from. I don't want to be clingy. I hate being clingy. But even more than that I don't want to be alone.

Alice leads me down a hall into a room and I follow her. Lights on. It's a kitchen. Warm wood, cozy, cluttered. There's a shelf with bottles on it. She takes one down. Gets two glasses. Opens the fridge. Retrieves something in a plastic bag. Puts things on the counter, arranging them just so. Pours the tequila in the glasses, making sure the liquid's even. Takes a half of a lime out of the plastic bag. It's gone a little hard. She slices off two wedges. She looks around. Finds the salt shaker. Turns to me.

"Hand," she says, and for a second I think she wants a hand with something but then I realize she wants me to *give her* my hand. I hold it out but she gives me a curious look and says, "Lick it first."

My heart skips a beat.

"What?"

"Your hand. Lick your hand."

"Uh …" I desperately want to do what she's asking but I'm also confused. Is this some kind of test?

"Oh, come on," she says, becoming exasperated. "Watch me. Like this."

She licks her hand slowly and purposefully, to show me, the back of one hand, the back of one slender, long-fingered, delicate hand, right between her thumb and her forefinger. I watch her with rapt attention, noticing the shape of her nails, the way she runs her tongue over her skin, and I feel a warmth in my belly.

"You want me," I say, trying to make sure I am very clear on what's happening, "to lick my hand like that?"

She looks at me and a smile flickers at the corner of her mouth because she sees something in my face and I guess maybe…she likes it?

"Oh, come. I'll do it for you," she says and she grabs my hand before I have the chance to protest, a move that floods me with an unexpected rush of adrenaline. I offer no resistance as she takes it to her lips, sticks out her tongue, and in one swift motion drags the hot muscle over my frozen skin. I gasp just a little. It hurts, actually. My entire hand is burning now that my blood is able to pump through it again and her tongue doesn't feel like a normal human temperature but like a hot blue flame that is melting the ice of my body. Tears spring to my eyes.

"Are you okay?" she asks, her expression unreasonably worried given she has no reason to care about me at all.

"Yeah," I say. The word comes out choked.

"I'm sorry. I shouldn't have done that. That was rash."

"No—it's okay," I say, practically begging her to believe it was totally consensual.

"It's for the salt," she explains, but she won't meet my eyes now. I can hardly believe it, but *she's* the one blushing. My heart is pounding like a hammer. "To make it … stick."

She shakes the salt from the shaker out onto her hand and it sticks to the wet spot which she holds up to me as evidence.

"See? First you lick the salt, then you drink the tequila, then you suck the lime. Okay?"

Check, check, and check. We both lick the salt off our hands while avoiding each other's eyes but I am looking at her super hard without looking at her. We pick up our glasses, clink them, and drink. It's my first time tasting tequila but I immediately love it because it burns my throat hot as it goes down and then I feel its presence invade my stomach and send out feelers through the rest of my cold, aching body. She hands me the lime and I see she is sucking hers so I suck mine, too. She is making a face like she didn't like the tequila.

"Dang," she says, after she has finished sucking. Her cheeks are flushed. "I think I needed that. Another?"

And what am I going to do, say no? She doesn't lick me this time—which is a little bit devastating, to be honest. Maybe I didn't taste good, or I didn't say the right thing. We drink, and the booze hits me none too soon, because my hand—the one she licked—really does not feel okay. Most of it is fine, or it's getting that way, but not my pinky. The rest of my hand is a hot blazing red that is tingling and prickling as it warms up from the outside in, but my pinky is white, white, numb, numb, cold. Hard. After I finish sucking my slice of lime, I examine my pinky, and there, at the tip, I see something has happened. It's like there's a blister or something but not exactly a blister; the skin there is dark and looks like a sausage that's been burnt. It's almost ... I know what it is. It's ...

"Necrotic," I say.

"What?"

Alice looks at me with confusion, so I raise up my hand and show her my finger.

"Necrotic. The tissue on my pinky is necrotic."

"What the fuck!" she demands. "When the fuck did that happen? When we were out there just now?"

I nod my head yes.

"Holy shit! And you didn't say anything?"

"I only just noticed," I say, slightly defensively. Though actually that's not one-hundred-percent true, because I knew much earlier this was going to happen, but it's only now that I discovered it actually did.

"Bring it closer. Give it here."

Flattered and submissive, I present to her my finger, which she admires in a way my finger has never in my whole life been admired before. It's really kind of sweet, like a funeral for my finger, like how only after you're gone do people realize the attention they should have given you while you were still alive.

"I've never seen anything like this before in my life. You've really got frostbite. Shit."

"Yeah."

"They're not kidding around when they say you shouldn't go out without gloves on."

"Yeah," I say, and I almost add, *or when you're off your rocker*, but I'm not sure she would get the humor so I keep that to myself.

"Well," says Alice, releasing my finger and leaning back against the counter and crossing her arms in front of her. "What are you going to do?"

"What do you mean?"

"Your finger—you said it yourself; it's necrotic. It's *dead*." She leans forward a little aggressively.

"Yeah, but—just the tip."

"Just the tip, okay fine, but it's a *dead* tip."

"Yeah, but the rest of it is still alive."

"So are you saying you want to keep it?"

"What do you mean, keep it?"

This is all happening so fast it's hard for me to keep up. Alice senses this and sighs, slowing things down a little for my sake.

"The tip of your finger is going to have to be removed, Kay. Now that it's dead, there's no bringing it back."

Now, this is something that is completely obvious, but I guess it didn't hit home for me until she said it out loud. I look at my finger, trying to assess the damage. The necrotic tissue only covers the very tip.

"Maybe it'll fall off on its own?"

"Uh-uh. No way. In cases like this you need surgery."

"Okay? So then … I guess I'll get surgery."

I'm not really sure what she's getting at. Why does she want to know so bad? Although, now that I think about it, surgery isn't really a viable option. My insurance won't cover it. They'll screw me over for the rest of my life for something like this, I bet. I'd be a hell of a lot better off just chopping it off myself.

"Let me see it again," says Alice in the commanding way she has. I hold out my hand and she looks it over carefully. I remember the way she licked me and wish she'd do it again. She pinches the skin at my fingertip lightly, as if examining it for springiness. She moistens her lips and for a second I have the feeling *she's going to bite it* and I'm scared stiff because if she does I know I won't be able to stop her. Then she looks at me with an expression that deepens the ache inside of me. It makes me want to give her whatever it is she's about to ask for, no matter how much it hurts. "Listen," she says, her eyes gleaming with an emotion I recognize very well but am too shy to voice. "I have a better idea."

Alice has a big, industrial-size paper cutter in her basement, and we spend half an hour cleaning and prepping the area. We have to make space, sanitize the surfaces, get gauze, and I want to drink more tequila, but Alice says no, I've had enough. It'll already be thinning my blood and we'll have to work to staunch the flow.

"Okay, but I think I'm sobering up," I say, unable to take my eyes off the paper cutter's long blade. "Are you sure that thing is sharp enough?"

"Should be. Come here. Let's see how everything lines up."

I walk over to where Alice is examining the cutting board edge. When I get close enough she takes my hand and slips my pinky under the finger guard and over the lip of the edge. She lowers the blade to line things up. We are faced with a difficult decision—where to make the cut. The tip of the finger is blackened, but it fades to a deeper purple before flaring into a raw hot red.

Alice slides my finger under the edge of the blade until it is lined up right between the purple and the red, right at the bottom of the nailbed. I think about how much it already hurts and how much worse it's going to hurt when she actually does it. I'm starting to get scared, to lose my nerve.

"Do you really think we should do this here? What if it doesn't go through? What if the blade gets stuck? What will we do then?"

Alice turns her attention away from the cutting board and looks at me.

"Kay, we don't have to do anything at all if you don't want to. I just thought ... but maybe it was a stupid idea."

"No, no, no. It's a good idea!" I say, instantly reassuring her, and then I have to laugh because obviously, no, it is not. My laughing makes her laugh, too. When Alice smiles, she beams. It makes me feel less afraid.

"What are we doing here, Kay? What kind of a world is this?"

"What is reality?" I say, echoing my imaginary therapist's earlier question.

"Reality is anything you want it to be," says Alice, stepping in and placing a hand on my cheek. Her touch is gentle, warm now, all softness and roses. Yet despite how inviting she's being, I have to push her hand away. I don't want to live in ignorance, blind to what's in front of me.

"That's not true. If it was, then I could say, 'my finger is an apple!' and my finger would be an apple."

"But do you *want* your finger to be an apple?"

"No—that's not the point."

"So what *do* you want, Kay?"

"I ..." I say, and I realize I have no idea know how to answer this question. Why is it so hard for me to answer simple questions? Maybe if Alice could just tell me what I'm supposed to want, then I would know. Am I just empty of desires? Am I nothing but an empty vessel? Am I unable to think for myself? This thought makes me so sad I could cry.

"Kay, what's wrong?"

"I don't know," I cry, and then I'm embarrassed because I just threw a fit and people hate it when you throw fits, when you fail to control yourself, and I am so out of control I am completely beyond hope.

"Kay," she says, looking at me with concern I don't want, and she reaches for my face again but this time I don't let her touch me. "Kay, just tell me what you want, and that's what we'll do. I promise. Cross my heart and hope to die. You're the one who needs help. So let *me* help *you*."

"You want to help me?" I demand. "Then chop this dead piece of shit off me!"

I thrust my finger at her. I slam it onto the cutting board.

I make as if to lower the knife and chop the thing off myself and she catches the blade handle and wrestles it up and out of my grasp.

"No, honey, no," she whispers softly, holding me to her. "Not like that. Not like that."

She lets me cry in the humiliating, sobbing way I have, my hands still pressed down against the cutting board's surface. What am I doing? What is reality? How do I take it all back and become a different kind of person with a different kind of life, one who doesn't suck? That kind of miracle doesn't really happen. It's just me, like this—pathetic—forever.

Alice gently lowers the blade back down against the cutting board. She puts her arm around me and holds me close. She rubs my arm until I stop crying and catch my breath. I wipe the tears from my eyes. I look at her. She's shimmering.

"Okay," I say at last, taking a shaking breath in. "I'm okay now."

"Are you sure?"

"Yeah. I'm ready. Let's do it."

"What? Kay, I don't know. I'm not sure if you're in a state to …"

"No. I am. I'm ready," I say, because I just realized something:

I'm ready to let go of my death wish—everything I was wishing for out in the woods. I wished for it so hard it almost got me. I was saved just in time, but next time I might not be. Everything I wanted has come to its realization right now in the tip of my finger, and once I chop that off, I can finally let it go. I can be changed. I can be different. I can be free of something that there will be no way for me to be free of otherwise. It's like Alice said: it has to go. But I get to pick how, and therein lies freedom, which is our only hope of paradise.

"Please," I say, afraid now that she won't do it. "Please. Alice. Will you do this for me?"

Alice's breath catches. She stares at me for a long time

without blinking and I feel like the air around her starts to glow.

"Okay," she says finally. "I'll be as gentle as I can."

I let her take my hand and line it back up on the cutting board. Every few seconds Alice looks up at me to see how I'm doing and if this is what I want. It is. This is exactly what I want, what I've been wanting all along. This is the moment I've been waiting for, when I can finally be free, when I can finally change myself and leave a mark I will remember, that I will never, ever, be able to forget. In order to be brave I keep my eyes on her face and I dare, for this moment, to let myself love her.

"Take a deep breath," she says,

And then she chops me apart.

NOTE FROM THE AUTHOR:

Kay's suicide ideation and negative thinking is inspired by my own experience with such thought patterns. I also know it is possible to overcome such thinking, and Kay's crisis represents the moment she arrives at a resolution to do just that. I therefore hope this story is helpful to anyone who might be struggling with such thoughts themselves.

THE FACE INSIDE THE CHRISTMAS BALL

DANIEL BUELL

"I wonder what's inside Christmas balls," Joey said absently to his reflection in the holiday bauble.

"Mrs. Bircher says it's how Santa watches us to make sure we're good or bad," replied Sammy. "Sort of like a camera."

Joey snorted before he released the Christmas ornament and allowed it to dangle on the branch. The ornament's weight pulled down the limb, sending pine needles raining over the Christmas-red skirt beneath the tree.

Outside, the sun dipped toward the horizon, casting long shadows over the snow-covered suburban streets. Every hour that ticked by was another hour closer toward Christmas—toward gifts and Santa. Joey tried to force down his excitement but failed. Fueled by sugar and his love for snow and gifts, he waited by the front door with his sister for their grandmother to arrive.

Like every Christmas Eve, Joey and his sister waited together for Grandma Allen to arrive with the wooden box of Christmas ornaments. The family had kept the box of ornaments for generations, though their grandmother would never tell the siblings much about them. She only said they were special and hinted at about some holiday magic, but she never said more than this. Christmas didn't truly start until Grandma Allen brought over the box of ornaments so Joey and his sister could hang them on the tree.

The idea of antique ornaments imbued with magic enthralled Joey, and he often fantasied about what the ancient holiday magic could be. Did Santa enchant the ornaments himself? Was it all part of some long-hidden holiday secret?

Finally, the headlights of their grandmother's car sliced through the darkness and flashed the house as she turned into the driveway. Joey waited as his sister rushed to unlock the front door, watching as Grandma Allen clutched the banister for support as she made her way up the front steps. She greeted both of the children warm hugs.

Joey took her coat and draped it over the chair next to the electric fireplace.

"George, Michael—" his grandmother went through most of Joey's extended family before calling his name correctly. "—I mean Joey. Come give me a kiss."

Joey stood on his toes and kissed his grandmother's cheek as his parents entered the living room.

"So Joey," Grandma Allen said, "what time are you going to wake up in the morning?"

"Early enough to catch Santa," he promised.

Every Christmas Eve the Allens would place bets on who would be the first one up in the morning. Joey would stop at nothing to beat Sammy. This year he would prove to her that Santa *was* real.

Joey had spent Christmas Eve morning devising a plan to capture evidence of Santa and prove his existence to Sammy. He thought and thought about how he would go about it, or if his plan would work at all. But that was for tonight. Now, he and his sister had an important job to do.

Grandma Allen laughed and mussed Joey and Sammy's

hair with arthritic fingers.

"Who wants to hang up the ornaments?" she asked.

The two children jumped to the task, each reaching up to try and be taller than the other. "Me! Me!" they cried.

Grandma Allen produced the familiar wooden box from her bag and held it out toward Joey and Sammy. "Come get your ornaments to put them up on the tree, sweeties."

Taller and quicker than her brother, Sammy ran ahead of Joey. She stood on her toes, excited as Grandma Allen opened the box to reveal four deep pockets. In three pockets sat brightly colored ornaments. One pocket was empty. Sammy picked the ball on the left, a green and gold-striped orb and rushed to the tree. She picked a strong branch high up and carefully placed the ornament on the limb.

"Your turn, Joey," Grandma Allen said.

Even though there were four pockets, there were only two ornaments left: a reflective all-red orb in the center pocket and a blue ball with snowflakes in the right. Joey could see his reflection in the red, shiny ball. He stuck out his tongue.

"Careful," his grandmother warned. "That isn't your face you're seeing."

Joey's nose wrinkled as he squinted at the reflection. He tried to decipher the differences between his face and the one in the ornament.

"But it looks just like me."

His grandmother's lips curved into a cryptic smile. "But there's a powerful spirit living inside of these balls—spirits who will take your face if you're not careful."

"Take my face?"

His grandmother nodded and tapped the ornament with her fingernail.

"These decorations are very, *very* old," she explained. "They have been with our family for generations and the story has been passed down along with them. My mother told me that if you drop a ball, the spirit inside will come out and snatch you up."

"Snatch me up? How?"

"A long time ago there were four ornaments." Grandma Allen tapped the remaining blue ball in the case with her taloned forefinger, then dipped her fingers in the empty space where the missing fourth ornament used to be. "My great-grandmother said her sister dropped one of these balls. Later that night, something took her from her bed, and she was never seen again."

Joey's eyes widened as he swallowed a sudden rush of fear.

Grandma Allen smiled at him, but she didn't look as kind as usual.

"Then why do we hang them up?" he asked.

"Because the spirits only come near midnight." She winked at Joey. "And only if you get caught staying up past your bedtime waiting for Santa."

Joey relaxed. For a moment, he'd been frightened, but now he understood. His grandmother was just trying to scare him into going to bed, instead of staying up to catch Santa. His parents must have put her up to it. Still, something in Joey's stomach didn't feel right. His fingertips were like ice, and the room had become so cold he thought he could see his breath when he exhaled. Maybe Sammy hadn't shut the front door all the way. Joey's frozen fingers worked their way carefully around the ornament as he ferried it to the tree.

"Pick a spot, shorty," Sammy said, snorting.

Joey looked up at the elegant tree wrapped in silver and gold tinsel and trimmed with star-shaped ornaments. Sammy's ornament was so much higher than his arms could reach, but he *had* to be higher. He pushed up onto his tiptoes, holding the ball by its string, and reached for the tallest branch in his path.

Careful, a voice in his head warned him. *Dropping the ball will let out spirits!*

Joe pushed the thought away. It was just his grandmother's old stories, trying to scare him so he'd go to bed on time. She couldn't even remember his name until she listed off everyone else's, so why should he take her word about evil Christmas spirits?

"You won't reach higher than mine," Sammy teased.

"I'll try."

Joey leaned off one leg, pushing himself higher, and hooked his ornament around the tip of a branch, pricking his fingers as he deftly worked the string around the needles.

The string slipped.

Joey's gut dropped to the floor like the Christmas ornament surely would. He would be the one to unleash a demon on Christmas Eve. He and his sister would be snatched up by evil Christmas spirits, and it would be his fault.

A larger, familiar hand caught the ornament before it could fall. Joey's father looked down at the boy and pointed to the branch he had tried to hang his ornament on.

"Is this where you want to hang your ornament?"

"Yes, please."

"It's not a very stable branch." Joey's father considered Joey's chosen placement. "The ornament might fall off in the night and break. We don't want that to happen."

Joey looked at Sammy, who stuck her tongue out at him, then back at his father and nodded.

"That one."

"Okay."

His father hooked the Christmas ornament on the limb and patted his son on the shoulder. Joey ogled the ornament a little longer before walking into the dining room, satisfied with its placement. He glanced at his grandmother, who sat on the couch stroking the family dog and staring into the electric fireplace. Joey hungered to know more about spirits and holiday magic in the ornaments and the evil spirits lurking within them, but he also didn't want to know. Christmas was supposed to be happy, with song, smiles, and lots of food—and not scary stories.

Every Christmas the family went through the same routine: Mom would set out the snacks, Grandma Allen would drink wine, and Dad would make sure dinner didn't burn. Joey and Sammy enjoyed the holiday festivities with full stomachs.

Nothing ever went wrong.

Grandma Allen's fingers brushed along the walls for balance as she made her way into the kitchen. Bent over, Dad peered through the oven widow to check the ham. Satisfied with the meat's progress, he began work on the side dishes and gave Joey the important job of mashing potatoes while Sammy watched snow drift outside the window.

When dinner was ready and the honey-glazed ham laid out on the dining room table, they dug into their Christmas Eve dinner. Joey found almost all of the roasted veggies disgusting, but the ham wasn't too bad.

He looked at the Christmas tree as he chewed his meal. The story about the ornaments and their evil swirled inside his head. How could a holiday full of bright things also have evil spirits that would snatch up children? Who would keep such horrible things inside Christmas ornaments?

Joey took another sip of the sparkling grape soda his mom had poured him and finished with a fruity burp, which earned him a scalding look from his mother.

"Grandma Allen, why would evil spirits be trapped in Christmas ornaments?" he asked.

His parents looked at each other and laughed.

"I see my mother has gotten to our son now," Joey's dad said. He turned to face the old woman. "Why do you have to do this, Mom?"

Joey's mother put a hand on the table and leaned over her plate, whispering in his ear as she smoothed away hair from his forehead.

"It's just a scary story, Joey. Grandma Allen is just teasing."

"It's the truth," his grandmother said. "Children must be in bed when Santa comes."

Joey sat up in his chair and leaned over his food. "Why?"

"Because Santa could knock an ornament off the tree and break one. If the evil spirit gets out, it won't be able to snatch you because you're in bed."

"But—"

"That's enough." Joey's mom waved her hand like she was swatting bugs out of her face. "You can't keep telling these stories, Grandma Allen. You'll frighten the poor kids."

"Joey." His father's voice was calm, but firm. "There are no evil spirits trapped inside those ornaments. They're just old heirlooms, nothing more."

"But what about the face inside the Christmas balls?"

"It's your own reflection, silly," his mother answered.

Joey considered his plate without responding, and his father rumbled with a low chuckle. "It's just your own reflection," he repeated, his large hand mussing Joey's hair. "Your grandmother loves making up these kinds of stories. It runs in the family. I remember when I was your age and my grandmother tried to scare *me*. It's not real."

"But the ornaments—"

"They're just old ornaments passed down through the family," insisted Joey's mother. "Nothing special about them."

Joey looked to his grandmother for some kind of answer or explanation, but she offered none. She simply sighed, then finished the remaining wine in her glass. Joey combed his hair back together with his fingers and tried to smooth away his frustration. Scary stories were for Halloween. Why his grandmother would make up such stupid stories to frighten him on Christmas?

Joey crossed his arms over his chest and melted into the spine of the wooden chair.

His father frowned and tossed a look at his mother.

"Come on, Mom," he said. "Why did you have to upset him?"

Joey's grandmother waved the comment away. "I didn't upset him, you two did. I was just telling him the stories my mother told me, and what her mother told her."

"It's all nonsense anyway," Mom said.

"It's the truth," Grandma Allen countered.

Joey's dad lifted his fork in warning. "Mom—"

"Do you believe it?" Joey turned to his sister before the

adults took over the conversation.

A wave of conflict washed over Sammy's face, but she didn't say anything. She looked at her parents, then her grandmother, and then the tree before her eyes returned to the half-eaten slice of ham on her plate. She shrugged.

"Samantha, dear." Their mom reached her slender hand to Sammy's wrist. "You're too old to believe in this kind of stuff."

"Christmas is about happiness and cheer," added their father. "Not about evil things. You understand that, right, Joey?" He leaned in closer and poked his son on the nose. "Is Santa a big scary man who doesn't bring gifts?"

"No."

"Would he want you to be all sad and not full of Christmas spirit?"

"I guess not."

"Exactly." Dad put his palm against Joey's cheek and grinned. "So, don't be all worked up over these—" he made air-quotes with his fingers "—evil spirits your grandmother has us all fussing about. Now, the sooner you finish dinner the sooner we can have dessert, okay?"

"Okay."

It took a large slice of chocolate pie covered in a mountain of whipped cream for Joey to forget about the evil Christmas spirits and the argument with their grandmother over the holiday feast.

Afterward, Sammy played with the dog. Mom and Dad did the dishes, while Grandma sat in the chair by the electric fireplace with another glass of wine and stared past the Christmas tree.

Had she seen faces insides the Christmas balls? Maybe it was just a story, but after his parents' reaction, Joey wasn't certain. The story would definitely scare all of his friends at school, and Grandma Allen wouldn't lie to him.

The Nutcracker filled the television screen in the living room, but Joey couldn't concentrate on the play. When the movie ended, Sammy fetched Grandma Allen her coat and their mother gave her a package of leftovers to take home.

"*If you drop the ball drops, the spirit will come out and snatch you up.*" His grandmother's voice bounced around the back of his mind as he watched her button up her coat.

"Remember to get a good night's sleep," his Grandmother said, and then with a wink, "You don't want to knock the ornament off tonight."

Joey's stomach tied itself into a knot. He moved closer to the tree and stood on his toes to gaze into the red Christmas ball. His reflection was distorted, his head cartoonishly larger than his body. His nose fat and round. The spirit, deep inside the Christmas ball, stared back at him.

It's just a stupid story, Joey decided as he leveled his feet to the floor. Grandma Allen just wanted to tell a story to keep him in bed. Yes. That's all it was. Tomorrow when she arrived to watch them open their gifts, she'd laugh and tell him it was all for fun. She'd apologize for scaring him.

Besides, Joey had put his ornament in a high spot, so Santa wouldn't easily knock it down like his grandmother warned. The spirits—*if* they existed—could not get out and he and his sister were safe.

Grandma Allen stroked her hand over his hair as he wrapped his arms around her.

"Merry Christmas, Joey," she said. Then, her voice dropped to a whisper. "And beware the face inside the ornament."

Joey turned to ice from his toes to his nose. There was not an ounce of enthusiasm in his voice. "Merry Christmas."

"Bye, Grandma," Sammy said before landing a kiss on Grandma's cheek.

Their grandmother wrapped her arms around Sammy and pulled her in tight, but her eyes stayed on Joey. Her eyes pleaded with him—no, *warned* him—not to do whatever he was planning on doing.

It was all lies. His grandmother had just made it up, he

thought, echoing his father's words.

When his grandmother had gone, Joey stole a glance at the ornament he'd hung, then stretched his arms and let out a great yawn. Sammy jabbed him in the gut, and he swatted her hand away, but she'd already knocked the rest of the air out of him.

"The first one who wakes up in the morning gets a special treat," Mom said.

This was one of Joey's favorite Christmas traditions. The first one who woke for Christmas would get extra candy to enjoy at dessert on Christmas day. Sammy won last year, because Joey had waited all night for Santa to show. Eventually he'd fallen asleep on the stairs. He woke up later that morning in his bed without a clue how as to how he'd gotten got there.

"I'll beat you again, snot-head." Sammy stuck her tongue out and Joey made a face.

"Yeah, right. I'll be up before you." Joey crossed his arms. "I have a plan."

"Sure you do," Sammy said as she leaned toward Joey. "What kind of plan?"

"A *secret* plan."

Sammy crossed her arms and looked down at Joey with a devilish grin.

"Do Mom and Dad know?"

"No." Joey shook his head. "Mom and Dad are always the last ones to wake up anyway." Joey looked around to make sure their parents weren't listening. "They won't be able to stop me this time."

Joey mimicked zipping his lips.

Sammy rolled her eyes. She flicked him on top of the head and blew smelly air out of her lips.

"Go ahead, butthead, with your 'secret plan'. Try it."

After kissing their parents goodnight, Joey and Sammy rushed upstairs and into their bedrooms. Joey would wait until midnight, maybe a little after, then catch Santa putting gifts under the tree. The key was hiding in the right spot. All the adults said if you're waiting, watching, Santa will know, and he won't come down the chimney. This seemed odd to Joey, seeing as how his family had an electric fireplace. So, if the Allens didn't have a real chimney, he figured, then the rule didn't apply. For a nine-year-old who wanted to embarrass his sister, the science was sound.

When Joey heard his parents' footfalls creak through the hallway and back to their bedroom, he waited an hour to make sure they'd fallen asleep. This time, Joey wasn't going to wait on the stairs and fall asleep before Santa came. This time, he would hide behind the couch and wait for Santa to come into the house. Then, *BAM*, Joey would spring his trap on the unsuspecting jolly old man. Well, he didn't have much of a trap, and he had no idea what he'd do once he caught Santa, but he'd figure it out in the moment.

Joey tiptoed down the stairs and into the living room. The only source of illumination radiated from the twinkling lights of the Christmas tree. Each ornament refracted the lights like hot orbs of fire, peering deep into Joey and scorning him for breaking the rules set by the adults.

Like a wolf or lion lying under the cover of darkness or a monster beneath a bed, Joey squeezed himself into the space between the couch and wall. Then, he waited ... for what seemed like an eternity. His mind raced with the thought that he might actually get his Christmas wish and catch Santa in the act. The big old man couldn't get through the electric fireplace, so maybe he'd come through the front door? Or would he somehow open the windows? It dawned on Joey he never thought about it before. The whole situation was rather peculiar.

The ornaments on the tree seemed to watch Joey as he blended into the shadows of the living room. The walls occasionally popped. The floorboards groaned and creaked, but he didn't hear her sister's or his parents' doors open.

He checked the time on the cable box. 12:03 AM.

Why wasn't Santa tiptoeing into the living room?

It's because he knows you're waiting. His parent's warning sounded in his mind.

That didn't stop Santa from visiting last Christmas, Joey reasoned. In fact, Santa must have been the one who moved him from the stairs to his bed.

Another thirty minutes past, which then turned into fifty minutes.

Joey yawned and rubbed his eyes. He felt himself drifting into slumber. He pinched himself on the wrist. Staying awake was important. He needed to prove to Sammy that Santa was real.

He got to his feet from behind the couch to steal another glance at the clock.

1:10 AM.

Joey frowned and crawled back into his hiding place. Santa still hadn't shown. He curled his hands into tight, frustrated fists. Then he crawled out from behind the couch again and scanned the near-dark living room. The corners of the room were swallowed by shadows and the tree, glittering and gleaming, seemed to pulse with some energy. Joey felt the ornaments watching him but was unsure whether they were spirits or cameras.

The floorboards of the kitchen groaned, and Joey jumped. No red-suited fat man with a big white beard tiptoed his way toward the tree in the dining room—but something had moved.

Joey wanted to give into the temptation of running. To lock himself in his room and avoid the spirits his grandmother had warned about. He still had a chance; he hadn't dropped an ornament. But there was something lurking in the darkness by the dining room table, and he could feel its eyes staring into his skin.

"Don't be a wuss," Joey told himself, but the thought of being watched made him shiver.

Feet pattered. Cold swept through the living room and sent chills through Joey's body as his back hit the door behind him. More footsteps. In the faint light that divided the living room and dining room, the dog swaggered out from the darkness. Betty's unruly white hair bounced as she walked, and her black eyes studied Joey. Joey's heart calmed slowed, and he sighed out his relief.

He bent down to give the dog a pat on the head, rubbed her back, and then watched as she climbed the stairs to nap outside Sammy's door.

Joey looked at the tree. At his reflection in the ornaments. He moved closer and reached up to the ornament he'd hung— or rather, his father had hung—on the tree. The branch wasn't as stable as Joey would have preferred to hold the weighty crimson orb, but it stayed put.

The face inside the ornament stared back at Joey, wondering why he didn't heed his grandmother's warning. Or was it thanking him?

Oh no.

Behind his reflection, Joey saw his parents, their arms laden with wrapped gifts and bags. At first, they didn't notice of Joey or even suspect to find him glowering at the Christmas tree. Then his mother saw him. She gasped in surprise that matched Joey's.

Joey looked over his reflection's shoulder, wishing it wasn't real—but it was!

His parents had carried the gifts—*their* gifts—from somewhere, maybe the attic, and were about to arrange them under the tree for him and Sammy to find on Christmas morning. His sister was was right: there was no Santa after all.

"Oh, Joey. No."

Dad's voice was filled with sadness. He stepped down the stairs, careful not to make any noise as he approached his son. Mom followed along, her eyes fixed to the floor and full of tears.

Joey didn't know he was crying until his dad brushed a tear away with the knuckle of his thumb.

"We wanted to wait until you were ready to know," his said.

Joey sobbed.

His dad glanced at his mom, who shrugged her shoulders. Joey let go of the ornament to hug his dad.

Crash.

Joey and his dad stared at the base of the tree in horror. The crimson orb that had held Joey's face was strewn across the floor, shattered into uncountable pieces. The gold-leaf top was split in half and rolling on the hardwood floor. Joey felt a wave, rushing between his legs, around his ankles, and past him toward the fireplace. His heart stopped and his jaw slacked.

"Oh no. Oh no."

"Joey, it's just a story," his dad said as he embraced him. "It's nothing but a silly old story your grandmother made up."

"Thank you," a voice, static-sounding in a rising and falling staccato, reverberated through Joey's mind.

The blood drained from Joey's body. He felt like someone had kicked him in the stomach. His eyes followed the hissing and crackling to the corner.

By the fireplace.

The shadows were thickest there, outside the light of the Christmas tree. Two eyes, like the flickering wicks of a candle, stared back at him.

Joey ran. He pushed himself faster, mustering what little energy he had left. As he jostled past his mom, Joey knocked the gifts to the floor. He cried. He screamed. He begged them to run and hide from the spirit, but his parents didn't seem to hear him.

His mother called after him, but Joey just ran.

Joey barreled up the stairs and fell over. He grabbed the stairs, not breaking his momentum, then crawled the rest of the way on all-fours.

At the top of the stairs, he scrambled back to his feet and skidded to a stop at his bedroom door. Once inside the safety of his room, he slammed the door shut behind him. He turned the lock. He grabbed his laundry basket and barricaded the entrance. Then, Joey looked around for something he could use as a weapon. He settled on the autographed baseball bat hanging on his wall.

Blood thumped in his ears like the marching of boots, and an army of blood soldiers thrashed around inside him in fear.

The spirit was coming.

His breath was rapid. His heart wouldn't stop slamming against his chest, desperate to escape whatever came next. Joey crawled onto his bed and turned on his nightlight.

"Joey, open the door," his parents pleaded.

His parents argued with each other. Then, they were sobbing. Pleading with him to open the door.

His dad's fists hammered against the door, but Joey didn't move. What if the spirit could take their voices and trick him into believing it was his parents? They didn't see the spirit, after all. No, he wouldn't open the door until the sun came up. There were only a few hours left. He could do it. He could make it until dawn. Right?

"There's no spirit," his dad said. "It's just a story."

"That's not true! I saw it!"

"Joey, please, let us in," his mom pleaded in a soft, emotional voice.

"No!"

Grandma Allen said the spirit snatched children when they were awake and supposed to be sleeping. Joey did the one thing he was told not to do, and now a child-stealing spirit was going to make him disappear. He wouldn't be able to say goodbye to his friends at school or tell his crush he liked her or get to work on movies when he grew up. Joey wanted to hug Sammy.

He clutched his baseball bat tighter against his chest and soaked his clothes in his own tears and sweat. Eventually, the fury died away. The small bedroom was full of dreadful calm and silence.

Joey gripped the baseball bat so tight he thought it would snap in his hands.

Joey didn't know when his parents stopped trying to get into his room or when he had fallen asleep. His nightlight was still on and his body was stretched out on his bed, the baseball bat laid across his lap. He yawned and rubbed his eyes before he saw that his door was still closed and barricaded with his laundry basket. He smiled. There was no spirit after all. Joey felt his lungs restored with hope and calm. Sleep called to him again. Joey decided that when he woke, he'd celebrate Christmas like nothing ever happened. The danger had passed.

Joey kept the bat near as he crawled under his sheets to go back to sleep, this time in comfort. He had braved the darkness like the heroes in his books and it turned out his grandmother did make up the story just to frighten him. As sleep dragged him into darkness, the image of the eyes in the corner of his living room came back to him. He heard again the static-like voice thanking him for dropping the ornament.

Trying to get comfortable, Joey looked into the mirror on his bedroom wall. He watched in the reflection as long black talons crawled out from the underside of the twin-sized mattress. The shadows in the corner of his room moved. A hundred eyes blinked and watched him. It was everywhere—it was nowhere. Joey twisted, tangled between his sheets as the creature moved closer to his bed in long strides. He looked up at the thing baring teeth that dripped with blood or slime, and he tried to scream.

He tried to move.

He was breathless. Alone.

His heart stopped beating. Surprise and terror slacked his jaw and widened his eyes, but it was his face reflected back to him in a thousand crimson balls that blinked in a slow, black muscle. The thing's skin was charred, scarred. Its incomprehensible mass spread over Joey, a sloshing noise drowning out all other sound as it folded itself around him. Blood dripped and fluid slathered over his bed and legs and chest until Joey couldn't see anything but *it*.

Sammy had woken abruptly in the night. The sound of shouting and clattering from downstairs had ripped her from a dreamless slumber. Something heavy crashed and banged as feet raced up the stairs. She groaned and rolled onto her side.

What a doofus.

Half-awake, Sammy connected the dots. Joey's secret plan must have been to wait up for Santa…again. He was so bent on trying to prove how real Santa was, only Joey's plan must have worked, and he'd found out Santa wasn't real at all.

Sammy's parents revealed the truth to her when she was a year younger than Joey, but he was too sentimental for them to do the same.

Mom and Dad were afraid of how Joey would take the news. Of course, they hinted that Santa wasn't real, but her brother didn't want to believe them. So they kept up the sham for his sake.

She heard her parents pounding at his door, begging for him to let them in. The ruckus in the hallway was garbled, but loud.

Poor Joey. Sammy rolled onto her side and went back to sleep, knowing when her brother woke up the next morning, he'd feel better for knowing the truth too.

Now, the sunlight streamed through her window. The clock on her nightstand said the time was 7 AM. Sammy stretched before sliding out of bed and opening the door to the hallway. The game of "who wakes up first" didn't matter anymore.

Joey's door was still closed. In a way, Sammy felt sorry his dreams had been shattered. She'd felt the same way when Mom and Dad told her Santa wasn't real, though she didn't throw a tantrum like Joey had.

Sammy had made a small pact to herself that if she'd ever have kids, she'll never let them believe in Santa, let alone some "evil spirits."

Still groggy, Sammy made her way downstairs. Her mom and dad sat by the Christmas tree, wearing matching expressions of concern. They looked up, startled and hopeful, at Sammy, but when they realized it was her, they went back to worrying.

"Is Joey's door closed?" her mom asked.

Sammy shrugged. She noticed Joey's ornament missing from the tree. Then, the broom and dustpan and the garbage pail. Fear seized her. She hadn't believed Grandma Allen's stories, but what if…*what if*.

"Did Joey drop his ornament?" Without waiting for an answer, she tracked up the stairs again. "We should go check on him."

Her parents followed her to Joey's door.

After trying the door and finding it locked, her dad knocked, begging for Joey to let them in. Joey wasn't a light sleeper, but he usually roused the moment anyone called his name.

Betty scratched at the door, whimpering.

"Break the door in," Mom demanded.

Sammy's father gave one last warning before forcing his shoulder against the door. The lock cracked. He gave one last, heavy thrust. Something clattered, and the door swung open. A laundry basket had been forced against the door, but it fell back as the family rushed into Joey's bedroom.

The first thing Sammy noticed was the open window. Cold air, snow, and sunlight drifted in. Papers from Joey's desk were scattered all over the floor. Her mom screamed and dropped to her knees. Her dad cupped his hand over his mouth.

Sammy followed their gazes to Joey's bed—what was left of it.

The mattress was soaked in a black sludge. A trail of it ran from the bed, up to his radiator, and out the window. Sammy crossed the room, stepping around the slime on the floor. The black fluid stopped at the windowsill. Outside the window the snow was disturbed, as if someone had taken a step into it, but that was all—a single step. No more sludge and no more Joey. To Sammy, it looked like he might have crawled out but then…

vanished. She searched the woods behind their house with eyes hungry to find her missing brother.

The police came quicker than Sammy expected. A couple of officers had the family gather in the living room while others looked around the house. Sammy had a blanket wrapped around her shoulders and someone brought her mom a hot cup of coffee. When they asked her what happened, Sammy didn't know what to say or how to describe it.

Maybe Joey had run off?

When they'd finished with their questions, the officers left her to her own thoughts.

Regret ate away at her, bite after bite. She sank her teeth into the flesh of her chapped lower lip and held back tears that pooled beneath her eyes. The last thing she called Joey was a butthead. Now, Sammy might not ever see her brother again. She couldn't tell him that even though she poked at him, called him names, and tried to beat him at everything, she still loved him and would trade herself to have him back. She just wanted to wrap her arms around him, hug him, and tell him everything was okay.

Sammy's mind swam with the idea of what she *could have* done. She *could have* stayed in his room with him and made sure he wasn't going to escape. She *could have* told him Santa wasn't real. She *could have* let Joey think she believed Santa was real so he wouldn't be obsessed with proving her wrong. Joey vanished because of her.

Joey vanished because of you.

The thought tore Sammy's insides to ribbons and she sobbed into her palms. Worries that she hadn't been a good sister bounced around inside her mind, and she choked on her own tears and pain.

Sammy got up from the couch and crossed the room to the tree and the naked branch where Joey's ornament once hung. She saw her reflection in the orb she'd hung, but as she squinted, something else emerged behind her. Leaning in close, Sammy saw another face in the ball next to hers.

Sammy peered over her shoulder, but all the adults were on the other side of the living room. She turned back, and the face was still there, watching back. She took the ornament with her thumb and forefinger and pulled it off the tree, lowering it to eye-level.

Behind her stood Joey, but not ... he wasn't the *right* Joey, was he? His eyes were black, and his skin was milky. He glared back at her, his mouth moving like he was chewing something.

Sammy gasped, and dropped the ornament, sending the pieces skittering all over the floor.

The air in the house turned stale. Bumps rose all over her body and her blood went cold. Sammy turned to see if any of the adults had noticed but they were still conversing with each other. They moved their mouths, but no words were coming out. They didn't notice the shattered pieces of the ornament all over the floor.

The groan from the wood panels in the dining room stole Sammy's attention. Joey was staring at her from the sliding glass doors outside. He pressed a bloody palm print to the glass and opened his lips, tinted blue and cracked. From between them, a long tongue slithered out and licked at the glass, leaving a trail of black sludge in its wake. Behind Joey was something Sammy couldn't understand. Something she couldn't fathom. The face she'd seen inside the ornament dug thousands of eyes through her flesh, through her soul, through to somewhere so deep and so dark Sammy didn't even know it could reach into.

A thing that could swallow up the whole world.

SAD LITTLE LUMP OF FLESH

ALCY LEYVA

As Kostia walked past the large wooden gate that led to the wooded area behind his parent's home, he took time to sink his tongue deep into the laceration on his bottom lip. With it came the coppery taste of blood, and of course a light pang of pain he felt ride up his legs and spine, but nothing he wasn't used to already. The sudden flush of his senses made the world come alive around him as he walked. He enjoyed these long afternoons by himself, taking in the creeping scenery as it morphed from the cold and rigid stones of his old parent's home to the twisty vines and crunchy leaves dotting his way into nature. He carried on him his big blue book bag full of materials he would use when he found a good spot to sit. These consisted of his usual art supplies: drawing pad, crayons, color pencils, stencils, and a fat eraser in the shape of a plane.

Mixed in with this bunch was a book with a glossy cover—Kostia's favorite book. The cover sported two dogs—a blond Labrador and a Yorkshire Terrier— galloping in a green field. The picture looked like the dogs were running right toward the reader and, during some nights, Kostia would dream this was the case. The book of dog breeds was his favorite, one of the first books he learned to read on his own, and he would take it wherever he could. Kostia, like many seven-year-old boys, wished to someday own a dog. And it was with this in mind that he had started going out to the woods every afternoon. In truth, the wooded area, with its high spanning trees and smooth rock formations, was the only place where he felt like things made sense.

With this being the first day of winter, the deep thickets cast a hollow mood over Kostia's walk. The previous day's rain had taken all of the crunch out of the leaves. Meanwhile, the bubbling brook Kostia had been accustomed to following was now a steady stream that reached up to the edges of the spongy earth and spun along like a big wet snake. Without the green in the sky above him, the sky was white and naked. The trees had extra spaces between them, and their barks had gone from lush brown to dead pale in less than a month. Winter was leaving its calling-card.

Kostia's walk took him through a small quarry where the stream made a hard right and came back up at the end. There were times when he stopped in this rock formation to find glittering stones to keep, but today Kostia kept walking until the path sprouted up again and the stream gurgled nearby. There he chose a direction and walked off, making sure to take note of a clearing where several trees had fallen into a heap. He knew to use this as a marker to avoid getting lost.

Twenty minutes later, Kostia was sitting on rock staring down at the earthworms that wriggled up and tried to tickle him through his boots. He played with them for a bit, tossing sticks and leaves in their way as obstacles, but then he unzipped his book bag and rummaged through its contents. Today he was dedicating to his biggest, most prized project—his own big book of dogs.

Over the course of the month, Kostia had created thirty-two pages of this book, all with his own descriptors and illustrations. He didn't include all of the breeds of dogs he knew, only the ones he felt were important. Whereas the German Shepherd, Greyhound, and Bernese Mountain Dog were obviously going to make the cut, Kostia left out dogs like the Havanese and the Afghan Hound. These dogs Kostia had no interest in ever owning because either they looked like a lot of work to keep or they didn't look like any fun. In his mind, a dog should run and bark and play. They should gnaw at your shoes and, while you should get mad at them for it, ultimately you come around to forgiving them. They should sleep at the foot of your bed at night to scare away the darkness.

Kostia had just placed the paper flat on his lap and skimmed through the book to find the next breed to include in his collection, when out of the corner of his eye, he thought he saw something moving in the brush. The leaves just to his right, beyond a tree that had rotted and broken in half, came to a stop. In his days coming out to the woods, he had never come across predators of any kind. He once saw two raccoons hissing at each other, but they only seemed funny to him. Seeing the brush shudder excited his imagination and he moved closer to investigate.

Jumping down to clear the brush, Kostia found nothing but a mound of dark mud piled up. A smooth stone poking out of its top. He reached down to pull out the stone, but instead of the hard surface of rock, Kostia's index finger sunk into gray matter like warm soup. Horrified, he jumped back, causing the entire mud hill to topple over and expose what was really inside.

What he had thought stone was instead the mushy bend of a small pale head connected to a round naked ball of skin smaller than Kostia's hand. Even as he held the dead creature, he had a hard time understanding what he was looking at. The roundness of the belly might have meant the small wad of skin and bones was a newborn chipmunk encased in mud. The reach of its neck could have made it a baby chick, fallen out of its nest. Its closed eyes were purple and bruised, and something grew out of its face—a beak, perhaps, or the first offerings of teeth.

Were those arms or wings? Was that a tail or a third leg?

Whatever this creature was hadn't developed enough for Kostia to determine completely. The mud and rain made the flesh translucent, revealing the dead veins inside like the empty trails on a map.

Kostia had no idea what to do with himself. It was the sort of shock that ruins plans and only puts one idea in your mind: run home, to a loved one, into a bath. Kostia ran back to his bag and hurriedly began packing away his belongings. A panic swelled in his chest as the woods around him turned wicked. Animal sounds went quiet. The trees stretched like shadows of whispering witnesses. In his rush, Kostia dropped a few items, but he quickly scooped them up and strapped on his book bag.

Instead of getting back to the trail—instead of running right out of there like a raging ball of fire—Kostia didn't move. For ten minutes, maybe more, the young boy just stood there— hands on his book bag straps, mouth open, eyes locked onto the brush and the sad little lump of flesh just a yard away.

The wind began to pick up and tiny wet flakes of snow fell on Kostia's nose.

Fear and panic ballooned in his chest as the seconds ticked by. By the time he actually moved, Kostia was shocked to feel his body walk toward the brush and not away. He ripped out two pages from his drawing pad and used a stick to flip the dead creature's carcass onto the sheets. He wrapped it up and stuffed the sad thing into his bag along with his prized dog book and drawings.

And then he ran. Kostia was running, tripping over stones and branches and slick leaves as the woods, fueled by his swelling anxiety, came to life around him. The rain hissed. The squeaks of his shoes pelted his ears like wails. The tree branches clawed for him as his body went into full flight.

By the time exhaustion turned his legs to stone, Kostia saw ghostly wisps in his vision, curling in the air. The break in his lip was now bleeding out onto his shirt and thumping in time with his heartbeat. He leaned on the wooden gate that connected his home's backyard to the path and gasped for breath as the full force of the rainstorm broke. His clothes felt like weights on his tiny frame as he looked back into the woods. He stood there, staring, hoping to God his nightmares were not coming alive in the daylight.

But nothing did come. Not a creature. Not a beast. Not even the skinless animal he had found. Only a roll of thunder in the clouded sky and the early flakes of winter.

Kostia closed the door to his room and emptied a shoebox, which he had been using to keep his rocks, out on the desk. The box was made of reinforced cardboard and he knew it could carry the weight. After taking a breath, he pulled out the wad of paper holding the dead creature.

Whatever wetness its skin had soaked up was now eating through the paper. Kostia had to use the edges of his fingers to tear it off. For a second time, he jumped back—this time from the smell that poured off it when the corpse hit the air. It wasn't terrible, in fact it smelled sweet and almost like strong licorice.

Under the desk light, the creature was still unrecognizable. Some of its edges were missing as if a rodent had nibbled on it overnight. Its crusted eyelids were shut, but the eyeballs seemed sunken out of their sockets. The beak or tooth, or whatever it was, was blackened. It reminded Kostia of a tooth he once had pulled because the root had died. Around the belly, wet patches of brown had formed. What it fur or feathers? Maybe both? Maybe neither?

He touched it with his finger.

The skin bent in a little under the pressure, but he could feel tiny bones pushing back against his index finger. Like a bag of water, pressing down on one end caused the other side of the lump to balloon. There was water inside? Could it still have blood?

Kostia wiped his finger on his shirt and wondered if his findings meant this was an alien species. The only other explanation was this was a mutated animal. He had read about mutations in his book of dogs, mostly in regard to their health and well-being. Even now, even this close, there was no way to tell how long it had been dead or how it had died.

Kostia slid the dead thing into the box and closed the lid firmly. Backing away, he stood staring at the box as if waiting for something, anything, to happen. Nothing. He made plans to bury the poor thing in a grave in the backyard after dinner, though he had no idea how to keep this event from his parents. With this in mind, he left the box under the lamp on his desk and backed out of his room, closing the door behind him.

As he turned, he could see into the room adjacent to his. Inside, his mother stood beside the shape of a man she was helping into a brown leather chair. An old radio played the news nearby. Kostia heard a man's stoic voice coming in over the light static. There was a storm coming, he said, and the roads and schools would likely be closed come morning. Both his mother and the man she was assisting into the seat seemed not to care.

With the frail figure now settled in the chair, his mother kissed him on the top of his head. Behind her, the moon had come out like a pale spotlight and turned the windowpane into a bright cross in her silhouette.

She walked out of the room wiping her eyes, but her demeanor changed when she spotted Kostia standing just outside the door. She wrapped her arm around him, kissed him on the head as well, and the two walked down to dinner together.

Later that night, Kostia went to bed and forgot to bury the dead creature in the backyard.

When Kostia awoke the next morning, he realized his parents had let him sleep in. Looking out of his window, it became obvious why. From his view of the backyard—with its pathway and stone wall, to even a large section of the wood's tree line nearby—the world had been transformed overnight. It was like nothing he had ever seen. There wasn't an inch of earth not covered in white.

From what he could guess, Kostia felt like a foot of snow had already fallen, maybe more. Thick flakes drifted down from the sky.

With school cancelled, Kostia felt he'd caught a reprieve from the pressures brooding inside of that building. He liked learning, and he liked his teachers, but all it takes is one person to make you feel like you don't belong.

As he tried climbing back into bed, Kostia felt a bite of pain in his shoulder. Sitting upright, Kostia could feel a lump the size of a silver dollar rising out of the skin over his collarbone. In the mirror, the bruise was a hideous blue-purple with tinted red. As he ran his fingers over it, a surge of pain billowed over, starting at his ankles and then coating his back and head. Kostia made small circles with two fingers over its topography as if he were reading in braille. Small, unending circles as he wore the pain like a warm coat.

He knew he had gotten the busted lip from what had happened in school, but he couldn't place the bruise. *Maybe when I fell yesterday coming out of the woods?*

Over his shoulder, he spotted the shoe box.

He realized with the snowfall outside, there was no way he could bury the box. Part of him wanted to open it up again and look inside, but Kostia shook off this impulse and pushed the brown box under his bed and out of sight. He would get to it when the snow was gone.

At the bottom of the stairs, Kostia came across his parents in the middle of discussing something important. He could tell by the way his father was standing, palms pressed flat against the dinner table, back arched like a cat about to fight for its territory. Behind him, Kostia's mom was standing in an opposing posture by the stove: head staring up to the ceiling, back bent backward.

Whatever they were saying stopped the moment Kostia's footsteps had echoed down the stairway. His father was there first to greet him and ask for help putting away the day's groceries. There were more than Kostia had ever seen: three large bags of rice; four stacks of canned vegetables, beef broth, and sauces; three whole chickens wrapped in butcher bags his father tossed right into the freezer.

"Roads are already closed going in and out of town," Kostia's father told him as he handed him a can of beef broth. "They say two days of snow, maybe three. Sub-zero chill to follow, so we're looking at an entire week up here. We're going to be cut off for a while, so it's best to be ready."

When the soup arrived, Kostia turned and turned the liquid in his bowl, watching the large chunks of cabbage bob up and down in the yellow fluid. Some of the salt from his first sip leaked into his busted lower lip and prickled his face like he had dunked his head in thorns.

Kostia's mind flashed out along the countryside, skimming the tree lines, until it landed in the crooked tree next to the dead creature rotting in the mud. The way its skin looked like mucus rolled tightly in tight cellophane. The odd placement of under-developed bone. The dislodged eye.

His mother's voice startled him.

"Yes, Ma."

Her eyebrows furrowed as she probed him about the cut on his lower lip.

"I fell," he told her, speaking into his bowl, "I was out in the woods and I didn't look where I was going."

As if to cut the tension, Kostia's father—not even looking up from his meal—asked him to bring a bowl to Gands in the room at the top of the stairs. Kostia did as he was told.

He crept up each creaking stair, balancing the contents of the bowl as he held it firmly between his two hands, and approached the room where Gands was quietly sitting in his brown leather chair. Kostia placed the bowl on the small metal tray beside the old man and waited for some acknowledgment, but it never came. Gands was in his nineties and could barely move. There were times Gands was talkative and sometimes even funny, but those days seemed to go with the sleep of autumn. Now Gands could only sit in his favorite chair, feet up, staring out of the largest window in the house as the snow fell just beyond the glass. Kostia's parents could not move him around so they kept him in his room all day.

This close, Kostia took the man in.

One of Gands's eyes was covered in a film of milky-white and greenish crust had started to form just below the lid. Dark pockmarks dotting his neck and his face, with its hard lines and deep paths, reminding Kostia of the bark of an old tree. Gands was dressed in silk two-piece pajamas with gold trim on the edges. The gloss of the lavender material clashed with the old man's skin, the moonlight giving it the appearance of pale stone.

The most unsettling thing Kostia always took note of was the smell that hung around the shell he had once called grandfather. It wasn't an unpleasant one. Actually, the reason it made him recoil so much was because of its odd sweetness. Not like candy or syrup. Kostia could never place the scent, but for some reason he disliked this the most. He remembered the smell from the box and how it reminded him of Gands, but he wasn't sure why.

Recalling how he could tell his grandfather anything, even more than his parents, Kostia searched for the words. Even in the enveloping silence, he could feel the man's presence in the room, like hearing the echo of some long-lost person's voice.

"Gands. I had a problem in school …" he said and waited for a response. When none came, he looked down at the steam rising out of the soup as if it were a spirit reaching out to him.

Kostia just stood there. Even with the snow outside being the only movement around him, he could feel Gands there, hovering outside of the shell propped up in the chair.

That night, two things happened in Kostia's silent home.

The first happened in the middle of the night. Kostia had gotten out of bed because of a sound. It was more of a trembling than a sound—vibrations that carried through the air and into his body. It was a walking dream that ripped him from his sleep and forced him onto the floor.

He thought the box beneath his body was trembling. He thought it was, but it wasn't. Not in front of his eyes, but in his mind.

Setting his hand on the lid, he felt nothing. Saw nothing. Just quiet night, black spaces in shadows, and blue snowfall building on his windowpane.

With this in mind, little Kostia went back to bed, not knowing that in the room across the hall, behind the wooden door, his grandfather had died in his sleep.

The next morning, Kostia's parents told him to dress and prepare. Later, as the snow continued to fall outside, his father came to get him in his room.

Walking from his room to the one across the hall seemed to take a lifetime. Kostia's blood rushed to his face as he clung to his father's leg. The process of entering the room stung as much as removing a thorn.

There was only one light in the room: a single candle in the middle of the table between the bed and the leather chair.

In the bed, Kostia's grandfather lay, mouth and eyes closed, his lean body still pressing weight into the bed springs below. He wasn't wearing the pajamas from the previous night, which meant his mother had taken it upon herself to dress him in the black suit he used to wear to church, back when he went at least twice a week.

She sat in the leather chair. She too wore black and her hair was now bound into a single braid she tucked in front of her shoulder. She didn't acknowledge either Kostia or his father when the entered the room. Her eyes were swollen and her cheeks, ones that in sunny days used to bear freckles, were scratched and raw.

The family of three stood in silence for an hour before Kostia's father turned him around and walked him to the door. His mother, a wretched statue of agony, never looked his way. She kept her gaze on the bed and the body in it.

In the hallway, Kostia's father placed both hands on his shoulders. He called him brave and asked to give his mother time to feel better. Kostia nodded.

Just as he was about to let him go to bed, Kostia's father added something else.

"The storm outside has buried the car for now. We're covered in snow up to the door. The town's snowed-in, too. That means Gands can't be moved until we thaw out. I'll try to make it soon, but you need to understand. Tonight you got to say goodbye, but that room is off limits. Do you understand, Kostia?"

The young boy nodded and said, "Goodnight" before closing the door.

As he pulled away from the doorknob, Kostia saw something odd in his hand and held it up to his face. The skin along his palm was scaly and rough. A pale film was forming—a scab. Searching his memory, he remembered cutting his palms when he had run out of the woods.

The box ...

As he changed out of his clothes, Kostia made a pact with himself. He had to get rid of the box beneath his bed before his parents found out. And there was only one place in the entire house he could hide it.

Kostia waited to hear her footsteps—those of his mother finally dragging herself to sleep—before he jumped out of bed.

By then, it was almost sunrise and the house, especially one encased in nearly two feet of snow, seemed eerily hollow. The wind whipping outside rattled the windows, but the rest of the house was as silent as a grave.

In the thickest socks he could find, Kostia crept across the hall. He held the old shoebox firmly as he pushed open the door across the hall.

Inside, the candle was snuffed out and the chair was empty. Only the cold body lay rigidly on the bed.

Kostia heard his heartbeat in his ears, and he decided to hold his breath as he stepped closer to the bed. If he opened his mouth it would free the pounding sounds from his chest and wake up the entire house.

Now a foot away from Gands's head, Kostia dropped to all fours and slid under the bed. It was stuffy and dark down there, but that was the point. With his hands shaking, he pushed the box into place—against the farthest wall and out of sight. Once or twice, he expected for the body above him to move or twitch, but as he slid back out and stood above it once more, he could see the full view of the corpse.

No blood to give color. No heart to give movement. Compared to this, Gands's state just before passing really did reveal he had life in him. He didn't move or speak, but Kostia always regarded his presence.

This empty shell in front of him was no one he knew. It was just skin and bone torn from life.

Young Kostia backed away and closed the door behind him.

The next morning, Kostia decided to sneak into Gands's room to check on the box but heard his father's voice coming from the kitchen.

He leaned back on the banister to avoid the first two steps from creaking just to get a better listen.

"Keeping that thing in here, in the house—it's unhealthy. We got a young boy walking around. How do you know he hasn't been in that room already?"

"That *thing* is my father," his mother protested. Kostia's mother stood with her back against the fridge. The color he had known his mom to have had faded. She still looked the way she had in the room with Gands—drained of life. There were lines forming around her eyes and lips.

Kostia's father lifted his hands. "I didn't mean it that way."

"And in what way did you mean it? What are you saying? Spit it out! If the roads are all blocked off and there's no coming-or-going, where are you saying we keep my father's body?"

The man shrugged and offered the shed in the back.

This made her furious. "You would like that, wouldn't you? You always hated him. I know. Even in his grave, you want to spit on him."

"He was terrible to your mother," his father shouted. "So goddamn terrible that he's been dead to your sister for years. We only took him in because he was sick. That's why I let him stay here. I held my tongue, but I'm not going to let you forget what he did to her. He was a monster to them. And what he did to you—"

His father never got to finish. The man shot out of his seat, lunging for the woman with such force it sent the wooden chair clattering to the ground. Fright made Kostia slip on the stairway, and he held his breath, watching as his father caught his mother's swooning body. The two collapsed to the ground, Kostia's mother sobbing and shaking. *He's not a monster, he's dead* she sobbed into his father's chest as he held her. He whispered to her and stroked her hair until she quieted.

Kostia went back to his room.

Kostia quickly learned it was a good thing he had decided to hide the shoebox when he did. He was a messy boy who liked to collect and build and never clean up. That's why there were socks and rocks and sticks everywhere and why his mother, once a month, took it as a solemn charge to tidy the space.

During this session, Kostia found her distant. Once or twice she smiled at him, but with the same blank and cold feeling as the snow looking around the grounds, threatening to swallow their little home whole.

That afternoon, Kostia sat at the table watching his father work on an old typewriter that had stopped sliding properly. On the other side of the kitchen, Mother was preparing chicken for the night's meal. There wasn't a hint of the morning's fight Kostia had witnessed, and he was thankful for that.

He marveled at his father. The man loved to fix things: carburetors, wonky air conditioners, old radios and typewriters. It was nowhere near his actual profession—his father worked at a bank—but a pastime he could never give up. What Kostia enjoyed most was watching the lines around his forehead bend, his cheeks growing taught under tight grimaces. He was a man possessed by fixing this piece of junk and he only paused to replace the screwdriver in his mouth with a few puffs of his cigarette or a sip of coffee.

"Why do things break?" Kostia asked.

His father chuckled to himself. "Any number of things can lead to them breaking. Mostly old age and wear-and-tear. Honestly, I don't know why some people keep things that don't work. Makes zero sense in my eyes."

For some reason, his father's voice grew lower and lower, as if the volume was turned down on him, until all Kostia could hear was the sound of his mother's knife working against the cutting board. Little white chunks of flesh clung to the side of the knife she used to separate the meaty pink blobs from the chewy fat. A pile of this unwanted meat sat on the edge of the slab—wrinkled membranes lined up as if in graves.

An hour later, Kostia stared down at what he had been served on his plate. The chunks of chicken clunked against his spoon, no longer pink. No longer the ball of grayish matter his mom molded and cooked into what his father was gnashing at with his teeth nearby. White stuffing. Splintery shreds of meat.

After removing the lid, Kostia turned the box over. The dead creature flopped out onto the dark wood cabinet.

He was in his Gands's room. Even though the sun was setting, Kostia could see out into the front lawn from the bedroom window. Outside, his father toiled and grumbled, all while making some semblance of a trench to dig out the car. The radio had said it felt at least 10 below and Kostia couldn't help but feel the world was flatter, more uncaring.

His mother, exhausted from cleaning and cooking, floated about the house like a phantom before his dad guided her back to the bedroom for rest.

The dead creature had spent only one night underneath Gands's bed, seemingly away from everything, but it was different. He had expected, after a day of darkness and less air, the creature would have started to rot or waste away.

But this wasn't the case.

The head and legs of the creature had remained in their same withered states, but the body had swelled to the size of a baseball. The skin, which had originally been pale and lifeless, was now blooming color around the belly. The smell had vanished.

Kostia held the lump in his hand. He had no idea how something so obviously dead could change into what he was holding. For some reason, it even felt heavier.

Originally, he was going to get rid of the creature, maybe even flush it down the toilet just to be done with it. But seeing the small changes happening on the corpse sparked a curiosity in him—a dull itch on the roof of his mind he felt he needed to scratch.

Kostia hurried to replace the lid of the box and get back inside the room where Gands's body was being kept. He checked to see if his father had finished digging out the car in the driveway. He watched as his dad, exhausted, lit a cigarette for himself and sat down on the snow-covered floor of the porch.

Seeing the coast was clear, Kostia rushed across the hallway and placed the box back under the bed.

The next few days, Kostia saw less and less of his mom. She either spent time inside Gands's room or in her bedroom. His father was pulling double duty, tending to her and trying to get the house shoveled out as soon as possible. Once, Kostia caught them arguing behind the closed bathroom door. His father was shouting at his mother for something she had done while she was sobbing in the background.

Afterward, he didn't see her for nearly two days.

Meanwhile, the dead creature in the box kept thriving. It seemed like every time Kostia lifted the lid, the sad little lump of flesh inside had grown bigger, more rounded. The tiny bones looked like they had grown in to form a ribcage, or maybe even the start of wings. With his fingertips, he could feel where their edges pressed so hard against the skin that the tips were bulging up like tent poles. The head and legs had dried to stumps, but the rest of this thing's body was now blushing with color. By the last night, the dead creature had swelled large enough to fit in both of Kostia's hands.

Kostia himself could only come up with one reason why this could be happening. He had heard of spirits leaving bodies when a person died. He had even heard stories of someone's spirit going into objects. Somehow, whatever he had found out in the woods had drawn in Gands's spirit. It was growing and changing because the man's soul was trapped inside. To Kostia, this was the only explanation.

Kostia thought about telling his parents, telling his mother.

Maybe if she knew Gands had a chance of coming back—maybe if this thing kept feeding and growing—maybe they could have Gands back.

Kostia, so excited by this idea, started visiting the box three times a day.

On the third night, Kostia didn't even wait to pull the box out from under the bed. Lying on his stomach, he removed the lid to find the sad creature had grown to be a bit larger than his hand and the blackened veins had retreated. Kostia passed the ball between his fingers, noticing the lump of skin seemed firmer. As he pressed in with his fingers, Kostia thought he felt a light flutter tickle his fingertips.

As he dragged himself out and sat up on his knees, he looked around with an almost triumphant glee. He knew he had to show his mom and dad what he had created, and he planned to do so the next morning. *Just one more night to let it grow,* he told himself as he turned to leave.

But there, standing in the doorway, was his mother.

Her eyes were sunken and the skin around them purple from her lack of sleep. Her clothes were dirty. More importantly, she had cut most of her hair. One side was shaved down to the temple. The longer side was browned. Her robe slumped off her shoulder, revealing most of her chest. She held onto the doorframe as if it were the only thing keeping her upright.

Kostia remembered his mother used to dance ballet and had the posture of a swan. But not the shell standing in the doorway. To him, what stood before him looked like a broken marionette.

The young boy was so afraid—of being caught, of the person standing before him—he couldn't form the words to explain. Then he noticed her eyes, those swollen hollows, were staring right through him like he didn't exist.

She stumbled past him as if he were a ghost. A pang of alcohol flowed off her gown in a wave.

Next, he heard the sound of a dull slap like dry meat falling on a tiled floor. Kostia turned to see that she had struck her father's corpse.

She struck him again. And again. Each slap sickened Kostia as if he were the one getting hit. His legs and arms didn't respond. He could only watch as she struck this body.

Until breaks in his cheek formed.

Until the sound turned heavier and more sickening.

Finally, his mother's hand fell to her side. Blood dripped to the floor from her broken nails. She turned slowly, as if on a rusted piston, and walked out of the room. The patter of crimson dots tapping beside her as she walked.

On the morning he was going to reveal his secret to his parents, Kostia opened the door to Gands's room to find nothing but a barren space. Everything had been stripped out of it, barely any furniture. The body was gone. The chair and armoire and desk lamp and radio—all gone.

Just an empty bed.

Kostia walked to the window in time to catch a white truck with chains wrapped around its tires pulling out of the driveway. His mother and father were there. He had worked himself almost to death to plow the driveway and the side of the house. The truck must have come from town because it had come with an escort—a plow truck leading the way.

Kostia's father held his mother as she stood wrapped tighter than a mummy in her robe. The landscape around the house had changed: the brown of the tree barks was coming into view, and the sky had thin ridges of golden sun tucked in its clouded folds. The frozen grasp of the storm was waning. The world was waking.

Underneath the bed, Kostia found the box. Part of him worried it had been taken as well. But it was there. With his hands shaking, he removed the lid of the box and looked inside.

When the bell for lunch sounded, Kostia—like all of the other kids in his class—packed up his books and stuffed them into his bag. He had left the dog encyclopedia back in his room. Weeks ago, he wouldn't have been caught without it on his person, but things had changed. What he had in his bag now was far more important than a book of dogs he would never have.

Lunch was grilled cheese and chocolate milk. Kostia slid these things into his pocket and went to the yard where students were allowed to play football and gossip. He slinked past these groups and found a quiet bench away from everyone else. The winter chill still nicked at his neck and hands as he sat down, but he didn't care. He sat and enjoyed his lunch and when he was done, he sat his big blue book bag on his lap. He knew he shouldn't—he should wait until after school—but he wanted to look at it again. He wanted to hold and examine it.

A kick struck him in the back of his head as soon as his hand sunk between the zipper.

The world rocked back and forth, and a high-pitched sound clogged his ears. When his eyes steadied, a large boy was standing over him. The boy was two grades ahead of Kostia and the reason for the busted lip he'd had before. His mouth was bent up in a snarl and he was saying something Kostia couldn't make out. Seeing this enraged the boy even more—he began punching Kostia.

On his chest.

His legs.

His back.

Kostia curled into a ball to protect his head. Each blow felt like he was being beaten deeper and deeper into the concrete.

Finally, the boy exhausted himself. His breath flushed out of his open mouth like smoke from a dragon. And then this boy spotted something—an object at his feet.

As Kostia looked on, wracked with so much pain that his vision blurred, as the boy lifted Kostia's prized possession into view. It was now roughly the size of a football and shaped almost square with protrusions and hairs in places. The head had completely broken off and was a stump. Bones hung limply off to the side, discarded due to the ballooning skin. The belly had stretched so far the hue underneath was black.

Before either of them could say anything, the flesh ruptured right in the boy's hand. Hundreds of black spiders poured over him. He screamed as thousands of black legs and abdomens and pincers covered his arms, his chest, and eventually filled his face.

By the time the adults came, the boy was writhing on the ground with red welts swelling up his neck and face—the product of thousands of spider fangs tearing into his skin.

Kostia, bruised and broken, only looked on.

A week later, Kostia took a walk past the stone wall of his parent's backyard and into the woods behind it. He hadn't been in school since the incident and wasn't sure when he could go back but didn't worry about it. His mother had been bedridden, weakened and fragile after the week snowed in, and she could not leave the house, but this too didn't weigh on Kostia at all.

He knew what he had to do to make his mom better and he set out that day for this purpose.

The woods themselves were different. The ice and snow from the storm was gone, but a second chill was in the air. Kostia led himself off of the path, this time far deeper in the woods than he did before. He told himself there were things to find inside the brush that day.

Broken things he could give a home to.

GLASS HOUSE, GLASS TEETH

TIFFANY MEURET

D raped in snow and gloom, a house loomed ahead. Waist high brush circled the modest home, clinging to the siding like a shawl. It looked empty—the windows were dark, vines long dead scarred the exterior, frostbitten to their roots because of this cold. An unnatural cold. It was the kind of cold that should have ended by now, but that was not why Em was there.

She'd left everything at home—her phone, tablet, even her car keys. She needed to make sure no one would find her before she was ready for them to find her.

Icy tendrils clung to empty trees, as if in a constant state of thaw and freeze. Em searched them for her reflection in the ice, finding herself stretched thin as it manipulated her features. Her reflection nodded, indicating the house ahead. A house that was never there before. A house that shouldn't exist. A house her reflections somehow knew was there, one which they pointed her toward every morning for the past three weeks.

Her reflections spoke to her in code, gazing toward the sky as she tried to put on her makeup in the mornings. At first, Em thought she was dreaming. She'd suffered from sleep paralysis since she was child, often living days on end in a repetitive loop until screaming herself back to reality and finding she'd only been asleep for a few hours. At one point the waking dreams occurred so frequently she couldn't distinguish between real memories and dream memories, as if she'd lived a dozen lives all at once. A dozen versions of herself existing within her, each slightly different from the others. Sometimes she was married with kids, sometimes not. Sometimes she worked at the front desk of a car lot, other times she owned a bookstore. Then she would wake up to her life, the real one, as her husband lurched out of bed at the sound of his 7 AM alarm and Em would forget his name.

"Which husband are you?" she'd once asked him, later blowing off his concern with the wave of her hand. "I must have been dreaming."

The first time her reflection misbehaved, Em assumed she was still dreaming. She was in the middle of applying her eyeliner, but when she'd lifted the pencil to her face, she found her reflection staring directly at her, one hand over its left breast. From that point forward, their hands remained placed over the same spot on her chest, as if to tell her something was wrong.

Not long after that, Em had gone to the doctor. Just to be sure.

That was the first day of snow, and now she was here, standing in front of a house that should not exist. Em had hiked this forest a dozen times and never once run across the house, and yet as she followed her reflections, here it was.

Surrounded by silence and low hanging trees, Em cradled her arms to her chest, truly considering for the first time what she was doing.

Then the door swung open with such force the wail of the hinges could have been heard for miles. A woman appeared within the frame, shadowed by the darkness inside.

Em froze, startled, as the woman turned to her, shouting despite the quiet.

"Well, are you coming in or not?"

Then she was gone.

Well *fuck*. Here Em was, cornered again. She'd been seen. Perhaps this woman knew she was coming all along, although if they did, they didn't seem all that interested if she followed through or not. Em knew this was her last chance to turn around and leave.

She also knew she wouldn't dare.

A boot-trodden path cut between the otherwise untamed brush, and Em followed it, wondering if she was to be the next missing person with her face on the side of a milk carton. Reaching the porch, she strained to see anything through the black entrance. From her place in the snow, the doorway opened into a hallway that dissected the house. Odd construction considering the house couldn't be more than a thousand or so square feet. It was the type of house that couldn't afford to sacrifice square footage for a grand hallway, therefore rendering the entire concept unnerving and ominous.

She stepped inside anyway.

The hallway was unadorned aside from a set of seven doors, three on each side and one at the end. Based on the size of the house none of these rooms could be any bigger than a standard bathroom.

There didn't seem to be anyone else inside, not even the woman that had called to her only moments ago. Every door was shut. Cobwebs stuffed the cracks in the doorframes around each door, none appeared to have been opened in years. Em thought about her choices while waiting breathless in that hallway. She thought about her dreams and her nightmares, the reflections that led her there, nothing but snow and wind for company. She thought she should turn around and leave. She might have had a normal life if she did. Instead she approached the nearest door to her right, pressing an ear to the heavy oak, listening. Nothing but silence greeted her, but as she focused a quiet murmur of conversation oozed into a cognizance. It reminded Em of the way her mother and husband whispered about her in the corners of her home, words she was never meant to hear, laced with secrecy and worry. Something about the tone of it, the clipped, assertive way the people inside whispered, triggered an instantaneous rage within her. It was the way a teacher spoke to a student, or a doctor to a stubborn patient. It was the way her husband spoke to her.

Her gloved hand circled the doorknob, and as it did the voices silenced. They knew she was coming, so she might as well stop screwing around. Expecting some resistance with a heavy, aged door, she yanked it open with a little more force than necessary so that the door swung with a bang into the wall.

Inside the room stood a woman, presumably the same woman that had beckoned her inside. There was no furniture, no windows, just stone blocks adorning the walls and floor. The woman was bundled within a thick winter parka, her face partially obscured by a fuzzy hood. Both this woman and Em wore identical, cotton black gloves.

The woman stared as Em stumbled in surprise, stopping only once her back hit the opposite wall.

"Hello," said the woman.

Em struggled to respond, tripping over her words internally until she gave up.

The woman continued without Em's participation. "Took you long enough."

"I was surprised," Em said. "I didn't know anyone was here."

"That's not what I'm talking about. Anyway, come in."

But Em didn't move, instead she gaped at the dark corners of the room. Gray brick consumed it, a prison cell more than anything.

The woman gestured around. "You don't like it?"

"What is there to like?"

"Admittedly, very little, although I will say this room at least has walls—a feat more uncommon than you'd think."

"I don't understand." Em watched this woman with growing unease. There was something about her that made Em's stomach drop. The timbre and cadence of the woman's voice strummed fiercely at Em's mounting anxiety.

"Let's try another, shall we?" The woman shuffled out of the room; arms crossed against the cold. She paused with her hand on the doorknob of the adjacent room. Muffled under the parka, she spoke in a low tone that forced Em to lean in to hear.

"Think of a happy place. Somewhere that serves as a comfort just to set a foot inside. Or short of that, think of the one place you'd rather be than here. Somewhere important."

The thought, no matter how much she tried to resist, populated at once. Em tried to fight it, sensing beyond all logic that whatever place she thought of, this woman would see. The urge to flee piqued to immeasurable levels. Em might have flung herself out the front door if the woman hadn't flicked the hall door open when she had, stepping inside a place she had no right to be.

Em had no choice but to chase after her.

"What the fuck?" she said. The woman stood dead center in the new room, Em's son's room. The walls were the same creamy white, his blue racecar bed askew against the back wall from where Em had to pull it out to search for his stuffed bear that had gone missing just last night. It even smelled of baby wipes and marker ink, just like at home. But this wasn't home, she wasn't home. Her son wasn't here, but that didn't stop her panic from unspooling in a long line of gasps and expletives.

"Who said you could come in here?" she asked the woman.

"You did."

"No, I didn't. Get out of here now. We need to leave, this isn't right."

The woman planted herself on the edge of her son's bed, shoulders erect, observant but completely unmoved by Em's anxiety. "He isn't here," she said. "He is at home. Safe."

"How would you know?"

"Would you like me to tell you? Or would you rather sit here and yell at me?"

Em refused to take her eyes off the woman. "Who are you?"

"My voice hasn't tipped you off yet?"

"Should it?"

The woman nodded. "You can't pinpoint, can you? It bothers you, but you don't know why?"

"The entire house bothers me."

"It should. Yet, you're still here."

Em placed herself squarely in the middle of the room now.

"You don't like me in here. You won't leave until I get out of this room," the woman said.

"Is that why you made it this way? So you could hold me hostage?"

The woman slouched inside her parka, as if exhausted by the conversation already. "I didn't make this room. You did. But yes, you called it right."

"Then tell me who you are. What do you want? Why am I here?" A slew of emotions battled for her attention, eventually congealing into a singular rage so overwhelming Em felt prone to physical violence. But it didn't last long, anger never does, and soon the fear once again buoyed to the surface. She thought of her son stumbling into the room, the woman reaching for him, grabbing him by the shoulder and posturing him like a doll to make Em do her bidding, whatever that might be.

"I have no interest in your son, Em."

Only then did it occur to her she'd never introduced herself.

The woman crossed a leg over her knee, settling in for a chat. "What did your reflections tell you to make you trust them so? They're the ones that led you here, are they not?"

Em dropped her hands to her side. "You tell me."

"God, you are so much more combative than I remember." The woman uncrossed her leg, immediately crossing the opposite before propping an elbow on her bent knee. "I'm tired of this same, stupid spiel."

The woman's voice had changed—she was less sure of herself, her tone softer than before.

"Who are you?" Em asked again. Her nerves were shot. She couldn't continue another moment not knowing who the hell this person was.

The woman allowed a lingering, slow leak of a sigh. "Fine." She removed her hood as if it had offended her, the same watery, brown eyes Em had seen in the mirror every day of her life staring back at her. The same hair crowned with unmanageable frizzy flyaway strands. The same off-white smile with front teeth that hung just slightly lower than the rest. It was her.

The woman was Em. Or looked exactly like her, in any case.

If this was supposed to be some sort of revelation, all it managed was to unhinge Em even more than before.

"This isn't funny. Who are you?"

The woman rose from the edge of the car bed, her shadow looming over the bright blue sheen of the molded plastic. "I'm me. You're you. We're the same, but we're not. Understand?"

She spoke as if to know that no, not one bit of that, made any damn sense. She stepped forward; expression unchanged by the way Em flinched.

"Stay away from me," Em shouted, regretting ever thinking this was a good idea. Just what was she doing here anyway? Following her disobedient reflections into this horror show as if they could help her. What was she thinking? They couldn't help her, no one could, not even the doctors—that's what they had said. But then she thought of her son, her only baby. She thought of him alone and crying in his room—this room—without her and she figured *what the hell?* What could she possibly have to lose?

This was not what she expected, and it isn't what she wanted, and she needed to get out of here before this odd woman and her odd house destroyed her completely.

Sensing the mood, the woman held out a hand. "Don't—"

But Em was already out the front door. Snow kicked behind her feet as she scrambled through the forest, away from the house. All she cared about was getting away, not bothering with specifics like which direction was the correct one to lead her home, to her family and her furniture and her normal house.

Just run, go, get out of that house. She ran without looking back, without listening for footsteps as the woman gave chase. Em couldn't stop. If she stopped, she'd get caught, and she feared if she were caught, she'd never again get out of that place.

Branches sliced at her cheeks and palms as she barreled through the brush—clearly, she was heading somewhere, she just didn't know where. After minutes she still had no idea where she was—nothing looked familiar. There were no far off noises of the city just beyond the trees, no sign of her own approaching footsteps in the snow even though it had only been moments since arriving. Then she noticed the spot to her right where she'd stood just before entering the house—but it couldn't be. It was the same small bush with the same icy branches, the same reflections beaming back at her as Em ran and ran.

But that couldn't be. If that spot was just there, it would mean she was still in front of the strange house, and with a churn in her gut she paused her scrambling just enough to glance back to see the woman leaning in the doorway, the house no farther away than a ten or fifteen feet.

Dropping to her knees in the snow, Em glared at the woman that looked just like her, knowing this wasn't a simple matter of Em losing her senses. This was deliberate, and the woman was clearly the one in control.

Not bothering to step foot outside, the woman shouted to Em over the silence. "You can run all you like, but as you might have gathered this is not an ordinary house."

"Then what is it?" Em crushed the snow under her palms into dense mounds. She was so stupid for coming here, and now she couldn't leave. Grief threatened spill to over, something she'd just barely kept at bay for the past few weeks, but as the moments passed, she realized how little control she'd ever had over it. The sensation dominated everything. She felt feral with it, nothing to cure it but the wild wail brimming behind her teeth.

"You're sick, aren't you?" asked the woman.

This acknowledgement all but destroyed her. Em nodded before crumpling into a sob, tears burrowing little holes in the snow.

"That is what led you here. The reflections showed you your illness, and then they brought you to me."

Em couldn't respond even if she'd wanted to—her throat was too busy struggling to breathe through all her panic.

"You aren't the first. Many of us have succumbed to the cancer you have. The only exceptions are the ones that leave or die before they get it." The woman breeched the house, her boots crunching through the debris and snow until she stood directly over the pile of despair that was Em.

Reaching a hand to her, she said, "Perhaps now you are ready to talk?"

Once again, Em was left to wonder what else she could possibly lose before accepting the woman's firm grip.

"Don't worry about the next room," said the woman. "I've already handled it."

"What do I call you?" Em asked, tiring of thinking of her as simply "the woman".

"I am Mimi."

They stopped in front of the third door on the right, passing both the brick room and her son's room. "My mother used to call me Mimi."

"She still does sometimes, doesn't she?"

"Only when she's upset."

Mimi led Em through the third door, entering a massive space decorated like a bookstore. For all intents and purposes, it *was* a bookstore, and as the door shut behind them Em could see no indication that they hadn't left their snowy little hill behind and traveled to a new place entirely. Flashes of pedestrians whisked by the glass front door, casting traveling shadows as they broke the warm sunlight peering through the windows. It smelled of mildew and books with a heavy tinge of coffee, though not freshly brewed.

Mimi instinctively wandered through the overstuffed shelves, settling herself behind the cashier's counter. Book posters, clearly lovingly handmade, littered the wall behind her. Em seated herself in a yellow reading chair placed in the small clearing between shelves where customers might sit and peruse their selections. It occurred to her that she didn't need to ask where to sit—she'd seen this place before.

Not quite sure of the impetus behind the statement, Em couldn't stop herself from announcing that she knew this had been Mimi's bookstore.

Mimi only nodded, somehow satisfied with this information. "You've seen it before, I take it?"

"In my nightmares."

"They feel that way sometimes."

It surprised her, though in hindsight perhaps it shouldn't have, to hear it spoken so matter-of-factly. No one in her life had ever just accepted them for the terrifying, dread inducing nuisance that they were. At best, people like her mother called her quirky. At worst, folks like her husband thought her disturbed.

"They ..." Em gesticulated around the room, hoping Mimi would catch her drift. "Kept placing their hands on my chest. The reflections. The same side, my left breast. No matter how or when or why I glanced into a mirror, any reflective surface, they were there. They didn't move their hands until after my diagnosis."

"They told you about your cancer."

"It's ..." Bad. Stage four. Invasive. Terminal. Em couldn't bring herself to finish the sentence.

Mimi drummed her fingers against the counter. "I can tell you the outcome, if you'd like to know."

"Do I?" Did she?

"Yes, but you wouldn't believe my answer, so I suppose it's a waste of time."

Em stared at her feet, watching the snow melt to the vinyl floor. She wanted to sprint toward the other room and fling herself into her son's bed. She wanted to smother herself in the scent of his steering wheel pillow. If she could stay there, then maybe he wouldn't have to watch her die. Maybe she could pretend it was a dream. Another nightmare in which she might awake.

"The mirrors do not speak until it's your time. They always watch, but never speak. We figure it's the smallest grace we could offer."

"How thoughtful of them."

Mimi snorted, though Em couldn't tell if it was because she was annoyed or just agreeing with her.

"So, am I already dead? Is this some sort of purgatory?" Because if it was, Em was fine enough skipping through the genialities and getting to the damn point.

"As if we would go to all this trouble for a dead person. My God, Em, how much patience do you think we have?"

"How am I supposed to know?" The words shot out of her with more angst than intended, but she didn't have it in her to care.

"My point exactly."

"So what are we doing here? Why did you lure me here?"

Mimi again rapped her fingers against the laminate counter. Em studied her as she did it—the gesture was as involuntary as it was annoying.

"You mentioned dreams," she said eventually, finally locking eyes with Em. "You've seen this bookstore in your dreams. You guided yourself directly to the yellow chair as if you'd sat in it a dozen times. Why do you think that is?"

"I don't know."

"It's because you have been here before. It was no dream. You've seen it. You've lived it. We have lived it."

"You and I?"

Mimi smiled, the first expression besides stoicism and slight annoyance Em had noticed from her since their meeting, and the sight of it chilled her.

"Us."

The way she emphasized the word "us" suggested she was expecting a certain reaction, one Em clearly didn't deliver.

"Sorry," she said. "Sometimes I forget you have no idea

what I'm talking about."

Ducking under the counter, Mimi rustled around in some drawers and cabinets, muttering to herself. Em heard the scrape of boxes being moved, one toppling over in her haste, before Mimi reappeared topside with a round mirror in her hands. It looked like one of those magnified mirrors Em's mother would use to help apply her makeup in the morning once her eyesight started to fail.

Mimi flipped the mirror on its swivel, each side of it a different strength of magnification. She lingered on it a moment as if deep in thought. "This was my mirror."

Then, before Em could comment or question further, Mimi hurled the mirror at the floor. Shards of metal and glass exploded in every direction as Em tried to protect her face with her arms, screaming in alarm.

She screamed again as she uncovered her eyes only to find Mimi dead center in the rubble, suddenly out from behind the counter with a dangerous amount of stealth.

"Look at this mirror," Mimi said. "All this mess, all these pieces, all from the same mirror, yes?"

Em sat frozen, aghast, and devoid of a response.

"They were whole, together, and now in one swift motion are scattered throughout the room. All the same mirror, but look where some of these pieces ended up?"

Kneeling, she lifted a bent piece of the plastic casing before throwing it over her shoulder. Then she dragged her foot through the wreckage, clearing a path through it with her boot.

"Some of the pieces landed across the room. Some of them you'll never find except to feel their sting as they graze your skin. These pieces ..." She lifted a particularly large, jagged piece in her palm.

"These pieces are Us."

Em felt glued to the tacky yellow chair, terror rising like a bile in her throat.

"Us—we—are this mirror. The same mirror, the same person, but splintered and fractured among the multiverse. Every breath, every blush, every blink and shit and fuck leads us further away from the whole. Our universe is like a liquid hall of mirrors, each of us rippling against one another as we drift and scramble through this hell. We aren't supposed to know about the others. We aren't supposed to see them or hear them or feel them, but we do. Us does. Your dreams were not simple dreams—it was Us. You found us, saw us, heard us, you *were* us. And now, you've come to us."

Em wasn't entirely sure what she was supposed to do with this information. It was garbage. Nonsense. It was insane. The things Mimi was telling her were so incomprehensible that her brain emptied. She struggled to form a coherent thought. It was ludicrous. So she laughed. This had to be a joke, right?

The moment was fleeting, for Mimi marked her displeasure at the laughter by dragging Em to her feet by the collar of her jacket. "I do not have time for your pitiful delirium."

She was so strong that Em's feet cleared the floor as Mimi thrust her toward the ceiling with little indication of tiring.

It was all so annoying and cryptic. Em dug into Mimi's hands, trying to pry her away, scared but also wildly incensed. "Put me down if you want me to listen."

Mimi smiled again, just as sinister as before. "Good."

As she touched ground again, Em caught a glimpse of the mirror shards on the ground—each of them stared back at her with a different face. Some stared back, some winced as if in pain, some had their heads tossed back in a wild cackle. All were different variations of her face, of Mimi's face, and all acted on their own accord.

Before Em had looked up, Mimi had made her way to the door again, holding it open and indicating Em to follow her. The hallway was even more imposing than before—dark and empty and yet capable of endless horror. It stilled her in place, not wanting to continue this sordid journey any longer.

"You can try staying here," Mimi said. "But I doubt your

ability to find your way out once I shut this door." But Em was no longer as tolerant of this hostage situation as she was before. Perhaps it was simply ignorance with a shiny gloss of confidence, but every defense in her arsenal was activated. The situation had long since spiraled out of her control, as if she had any to begin with, which was the exact thing she feared most. Cancer was out of her control. The future was out of her control. And now this place—somewhere she'd stupidly assumed would grant her some sort of answer—had taken every one of her deepest insecurities and stripped them bare. She simply wouldn't tolerate it anymore. She had to take something back, even if it destroyed her.

"You want something from me," she said.

"What is it you think I want from you?"

"I don't know, but if you are who you say you are, I can guarantee that you wouldn't screw around this long just for fun."

Mimi shrugged. "You're right."

Em snatched the tail of this sudden burst of assertiveness, unwilling to even breathe lest it topple her. "Then you'd also know I'm more inclined to let you shut that door and forget about me than be coerced into something I don't want to do."

"What can I say? We are stubborn fools."

"So, tell me what we're doing here, or I'm not moving."

Leaning a shoulder against the doorjamb, Mimi gave this statement as much concern as a loud sneeze in a quiet room. "If you believe I am who I say I am, then you know that if you waste too much of my time, I'll have no issue slamming this door shut and letting you rot. Hell, you can say hello to some of your sisters, for lack of a better word."

Em squared off towards Mimi as she tried to articulate her thoughts. She felt that she had already lost this standoff but wasn't prepared to cave just yet.

"Unlike you, this isn't my first time. I've been doing this for ages. I've been doing this so long that my children are now someone's ancestors in my time. Even though I am tired, I'm still better at this than you, and you know it. So, you can wallow here in your tantrum, or you can come with me and let me show you why we are here. It's up to you."

The rapid swing of emotions had emptied Em, leaving her feeling powerless and stupid. She would follow Mimi for a lot of reasons—because she had no choice, because it was why she'd come here, because she was tired and outmatched, because she was scared. But most of all, she knew she would follow Mimi into the next room because she was dying to know what it contained. She wanted to know, despite it all, she wanted to *know*.

Em stopped just short of Mimi. "How could your children have descendants when mine is still a baby?" He would be five in the spring. Almost ready for kindergarten. She had to stop herself there for fear she'd be swallowed whole by her grief.

"Time is a confusing mechanism, and not nearly as reliable as you think."

"Are they dead? Your children, I mean."

Mimi directed her to the first door on the opposite hallway. "They lived long, fruitful lives, as will your son."

Though she had no reason to trust her, it was comforting to hear all the same. "What's behind this door?"

Mimi smiled again, although softer this time. It struck Em later that this gesture was the closest thing to an apology she'd ever receive from Mimi. "Inside this room is the reason we are here."

And she swung open the door.

Em was immediately struck by the beauty of it—the floor was covered in a rust-colored red soil that billowed loosely around her feet as she glided through it. The ceiling—the sky—was a brilliant display of color, so vivid and unworldly that Em couldn't imagine any earthly image in which to compare it. There was a sheen to it, like oil over water, as if it were a living organism exhaling an inarticulate tincture. It left her breathless.

"We created this," Mimi said. A solemnity stole away the aggressive tone of the previous room.

"We?" Em asked.

"Yes," she said, pointing to a space behind Em. "We did."

She almost didn't see them at first—the other person in the room. Their silhouette was nearly invisible against the backdrop, but after a moment Em noticed they were coming closer in a slow, steady march. Instinctively, she took a step back, bumping into Mimi who had crept behind her so closely that Em startled as they touched.

"It's just a vision, so to speak. A movie. She can't hurt you here, but you need to see her. She has seen you now—the very second those reflections saw you, spoke to you, so did We. And when We sees you, she does not stop at anything before she destroys you and everything you love."

The figure approached more swiftly, as if hearing the condemnation and hurrying to prove it right. "Who are they?"

"We is one of the first. We created this house, this unending world that traps all of us. She pillages the multiverse for the ones she loves and would bring them here, leaving that person's world in flames."

"If she loved them, why would We ruin their home?"

The details of the approaching figure were beginning to materialize—the slope of the bridge of their nose, the grimace in their eyes, the way they clenched their right fist a little tighter than their left were all features Em recognized in herself. The approaching figure's mouth was masked, but Em could see the sneer underneath it anyway.

Mimi whispered the answer to Em's question. "To make sure they could never leave her again. For where would they go once their home was in ruins? It's smart, no?"

Em shoved Mimi away. "No! It's awful... It's evil."

Mimi leaned closer still, "And smart. Tell me, is there anything you wouldn't burn to the ground to keep your son near you?"

"Not if it meant ripping him away from his home and family, from everything he knows and loves, just to hold him hostage in my arms for my own sense of comfort."

"Look how noble!" Mimi shouted it to the room, voice

projecting far beyond what was necessary. "You're full of shit. Ask me how I know."

"I wouldn't."

"But you have. We all have. A thousand times over, we have pillaged and destroyed, and sobbed into the chests of the people we love most as we did it. Listen to your gut, Em. Listen to that fire, that rage. Don't tell me this comes as a surprise."

Em couldn't. She wouldn't. She refused, even as the recognition of those hidden vicious tendencies alerted her senses like tinnitus. She wasn't them. She wasn't We. She was Em, no matter how many times her other selves had proven otherwise, Em would never be that person. Now more than ever she was determined to prove them all wrong.

If not for her, for her son, who did nothing wrong but be born to her.

Em was so busy denying, so busy boring indignant holes into Mimi that she hadn't realized We's rapid approach. Before she could do anything about it, she was sandwiched between them, the shimmery, endless sky casting watery colors over the trio.

We leered at her, speaking in a gravely, unrecognizable voice. "I said the same as you. So many times."

Neither Mimi nor We paid any mind to the fact that We was changing—her hands elongated, nails stretching into excessive points, into wild, cage-like claws. They grew until they struck the dirt at her feet, and then, without warning, We rose up a hand and placed the tip of her index at Em's throat—the point so sharp that the slightest graze tore her skin, spilling a slow drip of warm blood down her neck.

"You said she couldn't hurt me here," Em said, panicked but afraid to move.

"I lied." Mimi shifted to We's side, studying the claw that held Em captive. "We can always hurt you. I'm sorry to say that complacence is a thing of the past. But—"

Mimi snapped her fingers. We was gone. The room was black again.

"There is no better time to show you what We can do."

Grabbing her hand, Mimi led Em from the room. The sight of the familiar hallway left Em gasping for oxygen. She's hadn't realized she'd been holding her breath.

She wanted to run again, to escape this strange hell in which she'd found herself. She pulled against Mimi's grip, but found herself woefully outmatched. "Get off me! Let me go. I'm done."

If Mimi heard her at all, she didn't say so, simply continuing to drag her to the next door as if she was no more than a heavy sack of laundry. Em's protests had devolved into nonsensical grunting as she tried and failed to get away. Her skin hurt, her eyes, her ears, as if this were the first time they'd ever been used.

The next door flew open without having to be touched, and Mimi thrust them both inside.

"Rage is a mutagen. It fuels us, it masks us, it gives us power, and sometimes we need that power. The rest of the time?" Mimi waved into the chaos. "This is what can happen when you can't stop it. When you can't put it to bed once it has served its purpose."

The room was nothing but smoke and screams. Em tried to see through it, but couldn't make out more than vague, amorphous blobs. Popping noises peppered the room, like gunshots but distinctly not any manmade sound Em recognized.

"Their bodies are exploding as the universe collapses on them," Mimi explained. "These are the final moments before their dimension is wiped from existence."

Shapes began to manifest in the smoke, dissolving and re-shaping the harder Em tried to articulate them. The sound was haunting and terrible, a new stain on her memory she'd never forget.

Mimi pulled her out of the room just as it was becoming too much. In the silence, Em could still hear them wailing. Em crumpled on the floor in the middle of the hall. All the doors were shut except the front door. Outside the snow still fell, gently climbing the sides of the house and spilling through the entryway.

Sitting at Em's side, Mimi folded her hands in her lap. "It's too much, too fast. I wish I had the luxury of easing you into this, but I don't. We has her sights set on you." She paused a moment before continuing. "And me. We is determined to reclaim her home, this house and everything else, and if she does, she will destroy everything. Do you understand? She will destroy everything. Not just this dimension. Not just other one-offs here and there. Everything."

"So what am I supposed to do about that? How is that my fault or my problem?"

"How can it not be? We is you. We is me. To know how and what she thinks is to listen to yourself. Just because you've remained oblivious all this time does not mean you are absolved of responsibility."

Em stared at the snow, slowly and reliably lurching its way towards her. Before long it would fill this hallway and bury her alive. Then what would happen? Would she die here? Would she blissfully freeze to death or would the house keep her breathing? Would We come and shred her body apart? Would We come for her son?

"Your son will live, but only if you leave him."

Em didn't respond. She couldn't.

Silence settled between the two of them, neither daring to break it. It could have been both days and seconds that passed, Em had no way of knowing. The mental gymnastics involved in understanding what she was being told overwhelmed every other sense. After a time, however long, Em finally faced Mimi, who looked as if she hadn't even bothered to breathe while Em considered all this shit. But the moment she faced her, Mimi met her gaze, her features relaxed into an exhausted sag.

"What am I supposed to do? I can't possibly be significant enough to change a damn thing."

"That's true, but only for you alone. I have yet to introduce you to our allies."

"Who are our allies?"

Mimi rose. "The rest of us."

Em gazed toward the last two doors, indicating towards them with a pointed finger. Mimi nodded.

"I have something for you," Mimi said. "The last door on the left. I'll wait here."

Adrenaline forced her to her feet. There was only an instant's worth of confusion before Em understood what was waiting for her behind that door. The slight smirk on Mimi's face all but confirmed it. Charging the room, Em stopped dead at the sight of it, almost not believing what she was seeing.

The room was perfect. Not just a recreation, not an illusion, but the real thing. The air changed as she crossed the threshold—he was just as she'd left him. Her son, playing in his room with his toy cars, waiting patiently for his mama to return home from her walk.

His tiny, precious face lit up as she entered the room. "Look, Mama! I found Beary Boy!" He held up his stuffed bear, the lovey of his that he'd misplaced the night before. He slept with it every night, took it everywhere with him. He'd been distraught when the toy had gone missing. A deep, withering sadness took hold of her body, but she forced herself to smile.

"Where did you find him?" she asked.

"I heard him. He was hiding under my bed. He was trapped there, Mama, but I saved him."

Forcing herself to be calm so as not to scare him, she sidled up next to her child, kneeling on the floor next to him and gently patting the top of his head. His hair was still crusted with bits of his lunch. He never could manage to eat without spreading his food in every direction.

"I told you we'd find him."

Pausing his play, he gripped Beary Boy in his little hands and stared up at her. "Where are you going?"

Em was taken aback, unable to stop her tears. Holding out her arms, she motioned for her child to climb into her lap, which he did without complaint. She held him tighter than she should have, but he didn't complain.

"I don't ever want to leave, baby boy. Believe me, but I think I have to."

She noticed he was hugging his bear as tightly as she hugged him. "Mama?"

"What is it, baby?" He shifted in her arms, turning to face her. She studied his beautiful, perfect face—his slightly crooked front teeth, just like hers, the slight freckles dotting his cheekbones, like her husband, his round, baby features slowly giving way to the little boy he was becoming. This was the biggest she'd ever see him. The man he would become might forever be a mystery to her.

"Take Beary Boy. He will keep you safe." "No, no, I couldn't do that."

But he was insistent, shoving the bear into her hands with a ferocity she recognized. "Beary Boy will keep you safe, Mama. You keep him." It was not a question, but a command.

Completely dissolved, Em grabbed her son. They hugged each other until a voice from somewhere else in the house broke them apart. It was Em's husband. He called to her son. It was time for a snack.

Pulling away from her, he scrambled out of her lap. "Daddy's got apples!" he said, but it was not her house she saw when he swung open the door, but *that* house. Mimi's shadow loomed over the floor of the hallway. Snow swept through the hallway, lacing the icy wind that carried it.

She screamed for him to stop, but before she could reach him, he disappeared down the hall, calling all the way for his daddy.

"No!" she called, stumbling headfirst into the hallway. Mimi caught her.

"He's not here," she said. "He's home. He's safe. He's eating apples as we speak."

Em tried to pull away—she had to be sure—but Mimi pulled her closer. "He is not here, and I need you to keep it together for just a few more moments. Let's go."

Ushering her towards the final door, the door at the end of the hallway, Em cast one final glance back towards the entrance. The snow had nearly walled it up completely. Only a sliver of sky appeared over the top of the mound.

"Once inside here, you will never have to hold it together ever again. Once inside, you'll have us. Once inside, however, you never leave."

"And where would I go if I could?" Em said, still looking back at the snow. Her son was out there eating apples. The snow would melt soon. He would play. He would grow. Whether she was here or out there, she knew now that he would be doing these things without her.

Mimi stepped back. "After you."

Without hesitation, Em opened the door.

Color exploded—the room was a gigantic jewel, every facet of its glittering surface a different face—her face. Mimi's face. *Their* face.

"You've met We," Mimi said. "Now meet Us."

Entranced, Em stumbled towards the center of the room as the endless faces followed her, each of their own accord. Some were scared and wild-looking, others serene, others even slightly bored. Before she could articulate the sensation, Em was overcome with it—it was like being smothered. She saw, felt, as the many trajectories of her life fractured and split just like the smashed mirror in the bookstore. What started out as a singular whole person was quietly chipped and torn as every possibility dragged them to different positions in the multiverse, as Mimi had put it. Em saw her childhood bully push her to the ground, and she saw every possible reaction a girl like her could have had, and she saw that cleave an entirely new person from it—one that made different choices, had a different a life. It happened again and again, until there were so many variations of her, she couldn't keep track of them all. She saw her marriage, but to different people, and at different ages. She saw her children, so many of them, all so different. She saw her child—*her son*—playing with Beary Boy, saw him losing his lovey a thousand other ways and becoming a thousand different men.

She saw her own demise a thousand times over.

Clutching Beary Boy in her hand, she faced the door again only to see that Mimi had not followed her.

Em expected it. Or rather, Us did. Nothing that had happened over the course of finding this house surprised her now. It astounded her that it ever had.

"This is Us," Mimi said. "Do you understand?"

The entire room, every possible face, whipped around to the sound of Mimi's voice.

"Us is a powerful creature, a conglomerate of lived experiences. The issue is that all this knowledge, all this wisdom and foresight, well, it can dull the heart. Lives become mathematical equations, logistics, probabilities. Us is an all-knowing guide, while missing the most important quality in dealing with humans."

Em nodded. "Humanity."

"Yes."

"Us needs an avatar. Someone still rooted to other people." Em understood so clearly it appalled her to think of how defensive she'd been before.

But that's exactly why they needed her.

"For a very long time, it was me, but now I'm needed elsewhere."

Deep in the recesses of Us, an image appeared. We was not the only one consumed with rage. There were so many—all of them understandable, all of them explainable, all of them a probability.

All of them threatened to upend everything, and it was now—had always been—her job to keep her own damn people from ruining everything.

"We is coming," Mimi said, hand on the doorknob. "I'll keep her out of the house. The rest is up to Us."

Em sat on the floor of the jeweled room, a thousand eyes following her every move. Stroking hair between her fingers, she said, "Don't worry. Beary Boy will keep us safe."

With that, Mimi nodded, disappearing behind the door as she gently closed it shut.

Em allowed her grief to consume her just long enough to be sure it was still there. Us swelled around her like a cocoon and cried with her. The moment could have easily spanned an eternity.

Instead, Em tucked the bear under one arm and said, "It's time for us to go."

And so, they did.

WHAT SHOULD APPEAR

N.J. EMBER

I f I never hear another Christmas song it'll be too soon. "Jingle Bell Rock" plays muffled and brokenly through the conference room speakers for the second time, and when it cuts off mid-verse I want to cheer. But I don't. I'm working and I have to be professional. Or as professional as I can be given what I do.

"Hey, tell me the truth. Just between us. This is all bullshit, right?"

I smile, pausing in the act of shuffling my Tarot cards. The woman is trying to whisper but fails. If I were an actual psychic or an actual Medium, like what it says on my website, I might have been mortified at the few heads that turn our way, but I've long since outgrown the opinions of other people, and this woman is clearly drunk.

I adopt my Stella Winters voice, which isn't an accent, just a little breathier and more mysterious than my usual tone. Or so I tell myself. "There are many things which are beyond the realms of human understanding. I only tap into some of them." I extend a hand towards the empty folding chair across the table. "Would you like a reading?"

The woman stills for a moment, going a little pale. When she clutches the edge of the table I don't have to be psychic to know what's coming next. I scoop up my cards and purse and bolt. She spills her guts just as my phone rings. I head towards the exit, dropping the cards inside my purse and check the screen before answering. It's my cousin/personal assistant.

I put a hand over my left ear to muffle the music. "What's up, Kaelee?"

"We've got a new booking. A house cleansing."

I check the time. It's almost eleven, which means my five hours are finally up. Note to self: never do another corporate Christmas party. A house cleansing? Fine. That was easy money.

"Cool. I'm on my way home. We can go over it then."

There's an unmistakable chewing sound on her end before she answers. I narrow my eyes. "That's not why I'm calling," she says, pausing to swallow. "Well, it is, but they want you to head over there tonight."

I frown, and not because I'm pretty sure she's been eating my snacks. It's late and I'm tired. "Now? Did they say why?"

"Just that it was important. And get this, they left you a thousand-dollar tip! No strings. Up front."

Up front? *They must be desperate.* "You're sure they didn't mention anything else? What did they say is wrong with the house?"

"Just the usual. Fritzy lights, things turning on randomly, sudden drops in temperature ..."

"All stuff that can be explained through faulty wiring or poor insulation."

"Exactly. Piece of cake. Go in, make nice, do your whole woogity boogity bit, and bam! You've got enough money to give me a Christmas bonus so I can buy the new JS palette I saw on Insta. It's purple and gorgeous and if it sells out before I can get my hands on one, I'll *die*."

I roll my eyes. "I think your paycheck is going to be a little light this month since you're going to have to use it to pay me back for all my eaten snacks."

Kaelee huffs, muttering under her breath, "It's just a little jerky ..."

"What jerky?" Then it hits me. "You've been eating my hunter's sausages? Kaelee, those are like ten dollars a pound."

Not to mention they're my favorite nostalgic stress snack.

"Okay! Don't flip out. You've just made like fifteen hundred bucks tonight, without the tip. Plus, I'm kind of saving you from yourself. You're almost *thirty*." She says this last part like I'm contracting some highly contagious plague instead of turning a year older. "You won't be able to eat this stuff forever, Stells."

I glare at her even though she can't see it. I decide to let it go. "How far away is it?"

"Twenty minutes. I texted you the address."

There's a high-pitched screech and I look up to someone setting up a karaoke machine on the makeshift stage. The background music to *Jingle Bells* starts up. Oh no. I draw the line at Christmas karaoke.

"I'll get an Uber," I say, heading towards coat check.

"Screenshot the details and send them to me."

"Always."

"And Stella?"

"Yeah?"

"Be careful."

The house was too quiet and colder on the inside than outside. That should've been my first warning something was wrong, but that's the thing about hindsight, right? I should've listened when Lila Ashcroft tried to send me away.

"You're too late," she says, her tone just as sharp and cold as the icicles hanging from the house's trim. She frowns as she looks me up and down. "And you're much too young. Go home."

I want to shrink at her words. She looks regal in a mint-colored pantsuit, heels, and pearls. It's odd she's dressed so formally this close to midnight, but they were expecting me so maybe not. My black velvet boots are damp and muddy from kicking my way through the unshoveled slush outside and I attempt to discreetly wipe them on the doormat.

Most of my clients are rich or well off. I don't feel right

about scamming them out of three hundred dollars an hour otherwise. I should be used to the initial scrutiny by now, but I always feel like they can tell I'm a fake.

So I try not to be stung by her words and smile reassuringly. "You don't need to worry, Mrs. Ashcroft. I've done this many times."

"It isn't a question of your competence. I just need you to leave. I'm not feeling well."

She shuts the door in my face before I can say another word. It takes a minute for the shock to wear off. I open an app on my phone, ready to order a ride out of here, when I realize I have no service.

"What the hell?" I mutter, walking to the curb to see if I can get a better signal.

No luck. *The cold must have killed the battery.* It's dark and I don't know the area well enough to walk somewhere. I look back at the house. My only option is to hope Mrs. Ashcroft will let me use her phone.

When I knock on the door again, it opens with a soft click. I freeze. Something tells me not to go any further. Some instinct that hooks me in the pit of my stomach and roots me to the spot.

"Mrs. Ashcroft?" My words come out in a squeak. It's been a long time since I've been afraid and I hate it. I grit my teeth and push open the door. "Hello?"

I step over the threshold, crossing my arms to ward off the cold. Goosebumps cover my arms and I shiver. I take another step into the house. The hardwood floor creaks under my weight, but I can't hear anyone. The feeling of unease in my stomach grows. Whatever is going on, I need to find the phone. I walk towards the living room.

"I thought I asked you to leave."

I spin around to find Mrs. Ashcroft standing behind me. "I'm sorry. My phone died and I thought I'd ask to use yours."

"So you just walk in?"

"Your door was open. I tried letting you know I was here."

There's a faraway look in her eyes. I'm not even sure she's really listening to me. "Mrs. Ashcroft?"

She startles, her eyes going wide. "The hauntings started in the basement, you know. Since you're here, you might as well do the job you were paid for."

The abrupt change in subject unsettles me even more. "The basement?"

"It's this way."

She turns around and heads off toward what I think is the kitchen. I follow her, thinking maybe there's a phone in there I could use. When I get there, she's standing in front of an open door. Soft, yellow light spills over the tile floor, but stops when it meets the edge of the doorway.

Mrs. Ashcroft doesn't look at me as she says, "The basement."

I look around but I can't see a phone anywhere. I sigh. I'm too tired to put much effort into my act, but maybe if I do this for her, she'll feel more inclined to let me use the phone. I cross the kitchen and stand in front of the doorway. Too dark to see the stairs. I try to use my phone's flashlight, but it's died in earnest now. It won't even turn on.

Everything in me says *run*, but I feel for the railing instead and climb down. The farther I go, the colder it gets. By the time I reach the bottom, it feels like I'm standing inside of a meat locker. I find the light switch, and a bare bulb hanging from the ceiling floods the room with light.

It's like time has stood still in here. There's a worn-down couch in the center of the room and a wall lined with old style televisions. The boxy kind with rounded gray screens. I wouldn't be surprised if the pictures were in black and white. A low hum goes through the room, letting me know there's a freezer or fridge running somewhere nearby. I don't take any more time to look around. The sooner I do this, the sooner I get to go home.

I take a bundle of incense from my purse and light it, walking the length of the room. "Okay," I whisper, waving it around.

"Whatever bad shit is in here, get the hell out."

One by one, the televisions turn on. I freeze. That's never happened before.

At first the screens just show the snowy fuzz of a wrong channel. But then, just as suddenly they turn off.

Okay, that's enough weird for one night. I don't need to know what's going on. I drop the incense, stomp on it twice with the heel of my boot and sprint towards the stairs.

Out of the corner of my eye, I see a man's face reflected in the screen of the TV, standing right behind me. He stretches out a hand towards me and I feel someone yank my arm, hard, pulling me off balance.

I think I hit my head. As I land on my back I look up. There's no one there. "What the…?"

Something is slowly dragging me across the floor. I grab the leg of the couch and whatever it is hits me hard across the face. I taste blood. I try kicking and punching, but nothing makes contact. There's no one to fight.

Ghosts aren't real. The thought comforts me right up until a pair of hands crushes my windpipe.

I gasp for air, rolling around on the basement floor. I don't have a plan. The panicky drumbeat in my head says only one thing: *survive.* I make it to my knees, inching slowly towards the stairs. I try yelling for help. As my vision starts to tunnel, I feel the anger rush back. The indignation.

Not here. Not like this.

I don't know if the words I hear next are mine or someone else's. "I've been waiting for you, Stella."

Right before I pass out, I hear something else. This time the voice is mine. "Let her go. This isn't about her."

I black out for a minute. Maybe longer. But when I come to, there's definitely someone standing over me. Someone with my face.

"Stella? Can you hear me?"

I blink a few times. I take a breath, and it's like I've swallowed broken glass. The raw burning sensation is worse than the time I had strep throat. I still try to say the word anyway. And when that fails, I mouth it. *"CeeCee?"*

She smiles. "I knew you'd remember."

Of course I remember. But are your imaginary friends supposed to age with you? Or look cooler than you? Because Celia did.

"Don't overthink it. It isn't important," she says. The light flickers above us and she tenses. She grabs a crowbar that's lying next to her. "The only thing that matters right now is that you run as fast as you can up those stairs. Can you do that?"

I whimper softly, shaking my head. It hurts to move. It hurts to breathe.

CeeCee takes my hand. "You have to try, Stella, okay? I'm sorry, but it's the only way."

She pulls me to my feet. The room tilts, but it sharpens for a fraction of a second as I'm shoved towards the stairs. They're the kind with no riser, and I don't trust myself to stand, so I grasp the back of each one and crawl as fast as I can towards the top. I'm two steps away when someone reaches up from underneath me and tries to pull me back down. I stretch my hand out for the next one, desperately pulling as the air evaporates from my lungs. I'm too weak. I feel myself slip down a stair.

"No," I say, warm tears spilling out. "Someone help!"

Lila's at the top of the stairs, bending down and reaching for me. I reach out with both hands. This is my last chance. As she grabs my hands, whatever's holding me squeezes and I pass out.

When I open my eyes again, I'm staring at a ceiling. I can hear the honking of car horns outside. She must have dragged me into the hallway. I lift my head and meet her eyes. "I think you should move," I rasp.

She smiles. By now, we both know that's an understatement.

"It's too late for that. I tried to tell you."

She stares at something in the living room. Something I can't quite see. I turn over, crawl a little further, peering around the doorway. I scream.

She couldn't have dragged me anywhere. Not up the basement steps. Not into the hallway. On the sofa, sitting in front of the television are Lila Ashcroft and what has to be her husband. Their eyes are open, staring at nothing. Seeing nothing.

Because they're both dead.

Every child wants to feel safe. I had a therapist tell me that once and it stuck with me ever since. Parents lie to their kids all the time, so they do. They tell us there's nothing under our beds. They tell us there's nothing waiting in the dark. There's no such thing as monsters. But now I've seen things.

I've been asleep before this. I've been asleep, and now that I'm awake the world looks different. Or have I fallen into a nightmare instead?

I stare at my hands. At the splint they've wrapped around two of my discolored fingers. The doctor says they're broken. Only I know they were broken by someone I couldn't see. So how do I answer their questions? The doctors, the police, the nurses all ask the same things: what happened? Who hurt me?

But I know they won't believe me. If it weren't for the injuries, I might've been able to go back to disbelief myself. I might have been able to go back to feeling safe again.

"I still can't believe you were able to call for help. The way your throat is? That's a miracle if ever there was one," says the nurse who has been taking care of me.

I think her name is Belinda or Melinda. I wasn't really paying attention when she told me, and I don't want to seem rude by asking her again. She finishes taking my vitals and sets a notepad and pen in front of me. "Someone is on the way to pick you up. Whoever you listed as your emergency contact. The roads are bad, so it might be awhile. Until then, just try to relax. Maybe take a nap. If you need anything just push your call button."

I give her a thumb's up in response, but I know I won't be able to sleep. Because I wasn't the one who had called for help. When I saw the Ashcroft's bodies, I gathered up whatever strength I had left and ran from the house. I'd collapsed on the front lawn, curled up in the snow, and stared at the Christmas lights on the house across the street until an ambulance pulled up and took me to the hospital.

CeeCee had to be the one who made the call. But that was another unexplainable thing. How could my imaginary friend be real? How had she known to help me? The last time I'd seen her I'd been eight, six months after my parents died. My therapist told my aunt that she was a normal response to my trauma.

Is that all she was now? But she couldn't be, because she'd held my hand in the basement and helped me to the stairs. She'd felt solid, real, flesh and blood. *But so had Lila Ashcroft.* Except I'd never really felt her touch me.

I was so exhausted I wished I could sleep. I needed help. Someone I could talk to about all this who wouldn't think I was crazy. Someone who might have answers. As much as I hated the idea of it, I needed a real Medium. But that would mean going to see...

"Stella?"

Kaelee's here. Her face is red and blotchy, so I can tell she's been crying. She approaches me carefully, slowly and without meeting my eyes. When she finally makes it to the side of the bed, I take her hand and give it a squeeze. She starts crying again, quietly, which is so unlike her I start to worry.

I pick up the notepad and pen. I'm not going to attempt talking right now. It hurts and I don't want to startle her with my scary rasp. *What's wrong?*

I hold up the notepad so she can see it. Kaelee makes this weird squeak, somewhere between a laugh and a yell. "What's wrong? Stella, look at you! You're all bruised and bandaged. You look *awful*."

I glare at her, and this time she can see it. Instead of looking apologetic, she laughs. "Okay. Probably not the best thing to say right now, but you do. And it's my fault."

My eyes widen in sock. Her fault? I grab the notepad again, writing so fast some of my letters smush together. I underline the first word twice. *Not your fault. It was my decision to go.*

"But I pushed you. I told you it would be no big deal, even though we usually do way more research on potential clients before you do the job. I hadn't even vetted them properly. I got caught up because of the extra money."

I wave my hands at her words as if they're made of smoke. As if I can extinguish her guilt that easily. I scribble on the notepad again. *We both liked the idea of extra money.*

"I'm your assistant. I'm supposed to help you and make things easier on you. Not get you hurt."

You're my family and I love you.

That's what's most important. It was also why I couldn't tell her the truth.

"Are you sure about this?" Kaelee asks me for the millionth time since I asked her to look up the address four days ago. I don't bother answering as I climb out of the car.

The truthful answer is no. The only person who can help me is the last person I want to see, let alone ask for help. It isn't that I have anything against Gideon Gray, but the last time we were in a room together, I hadn't exactly charmed my way on to his Christmas card list.

Yet, here I was, kicking through slush again and sidestepping the pile of damp, unopened mail on his porch to knock on his door. No one answered.

"Mr. Gray," I yell and knock again. I glance at the pile of mail. *Maybe he's not home. Or on vacation.*

Kaelee's idling by the curb, and I glance over my shoulder. I could give up. I could try to move on with my life and pretend like this never happened. Except every night I dream of Lila Ashcroft's glassy dead eyes staring at me, while another version of her stands over me, telling me, "Go away, Stella."

Every time I wake, I'm left with questions I can't answer. If the Ashcroft's had been dead before I got there, then was it really them Kaelee talked to over the phone? If Lila was dead, was it really her ghost that'd answered the door? Her ghost that lead me into the basement?

What was it that had attacked me in the basement? I'd seen a man's face, and in the worst of my nightmares I could still hear him laughing. I could still feel his hands squeezing my throat as I woke up gasping for breath.

Then there's CeeCee. She was the most real thing in the house. Was she really my imaginary friend brought to life somehow? Or was she something else. The internet search I did gave me another answer: doppelgänger. But the internet also said that if CeeCee was my doppelgänger then seeing her meant only one thing for sure. I'm going to die.

I kick the door in frustration. I can't let this go.

The door swings open. "Alright, alright, already. Was that really necessary? Do you have to try and kick down my door so early in the morning?"

I frown and check my phone. "It's past noon."

The man standing in front of me shrugs. He's wearing sunglasses, his light blue cardigan rumpled like he'd slept in it, the collar of a white t-shirt peeking out underneath. His hair is pure white despite a younger face, I'd guess mid-forties. Gideon Gray looks the same as he had two years ago, but judging from the whiff of stale drink coming off of him I don't think they'd been kind.

"Listen, Honey, I don't want any cookies alright? But thanks anyway." He moves to shut the door.

Panic rises up in me. I grab on to the frame. "Girl Scout season was three months ago."

He gives me a wry smile, glancing at my hand. "That's my nice way of saying whatever it is you're selling, I'm not buying."

"I'm not selling anything. I'm here for your help, Mr. Gray."

He frowns and his brow furrows. He opens the door a little more. "My help?"

I hesitate, but it's now or never. "I can tell you don't remember me. My name is Stella Tolliver. You'd know me as Stella Winters."

His face darkens. I continue in a rush before he can say or do anything else. "A week ago I was attacked by what I think was a ghost."

He laughs flatly. "I'd like you to get off my property, Ms. Winters. Now."

I won't be sent away again. The memory of Lila is still too fresh in my mind. There's only one thing left to do. I rip off my scarf. The bruises have faded a little, not so black as they were, tinged green in places, but they're still there. Long splotches wrapping around my throat, like fingers. "It killed two of my clients. It almost killed me. Please. I don't have anyone else who can help me."

"Jesus," he says.

"I know you have every right to hate me—"

Gideon cuts me off. "Oh, you mean for ruining my career? For telling everyone I was a fraud? No. Why would I hate you for that?"

"I'm sorry," I say, flinching. "I know an apology won't make up for everything that's happened. I know you don't have any reason to believe me, but please just let me explain."

He stares at me for a second, taking in my words and my injuries, his eyes darting to the splint on my broken fingers. He moves aside. "Ten minutes. No promises."

Gideon nods towards the living room and I take a seat on the sofa. Empty food wrappers, dirty dishes and books litter the space. We avoid eye contact with each other as he gathers up empty liquor bottles and glasses, clearing the coffee table that separates us. When that's done, he takes the armchair opposite me, a fresh glass of scotch in his hand.

"Your ten minutes start now," he says, sipping from the glass.

So I tell him everything. I tell him about the tip with no strings, about Lila Ashcroft's warning, about as much as I can remember from what happened in the basement. I even tell him about CeeCee, but I don't tell him who she is. I need him to help me and one unbelievable thing at a time is enough.

"Lila Ashcroft was dead all that time, so she can't have been the one who let me into the house, unless she was a ghost. That's not possible, is it?" I ask as I finish the story.

Gideon's glass is empty. He upended it when I told him how I had discovered the bodies. He looks from it to me. "It's unlikely but not impossible. Do you know how long the Ashcrofts lived in that house?"

I shake my head as Gideon gets up to refill his glass. "Research is important. There's key things you should know about your clients before you work with them."

"But isn't that dishonest? As a Medium, shouldn't you know things about people without researching them beforehand?"

Gideon chuckles as he pours, shaking his head. "Still think I'm a fraud, Stella?" He puts up a hand when I start to speak. "I said key things, not everything. It's about safety. Group events or larger venues are different because they'll have security. But going into someone's home? If you'd known more about the Ashcroft's beforehand, you might have prepared differently."

I don't say anything. Kaelee had made that same point.

Gideon continues. "Going back to Lila Ashcroft—a person who has passed on after living in the house for an extended time will have a stronger attachment to the house, so sometimes their spirit is able to do more. Have more of an effect on their surroundings."

"So that's why Lila's spirit was able to appear so normal."

"That," says Gideon, taking his seat again. "Or another reason."

"Another reason?"

Gideon nods. "From everything you told me, I don't think

the Ashcroft's were running the show in that house at all. I think there's another spirit, someone who lived there longer, has been dead longer and has serious juice. A darker spirit. I think it lured you there."

I shiver as icy dread creeps up the back of my neck. "Why? What would it want with me?"

"That I don't know. Some spirits are mean and malicious in death because they were that way in life. Some go bad over time like expired milk, pissed off at the way they died. They're unable to move on. Each spirit was once a person, so just like people they have their own reasons."

"So, I have to find out what it wants with me before I can get rid of it."

"No. You need to stay as far away from that house as possible," Gideon says. "Weren't you listening? It lured you there, and then it tried to kill you. Your job is done."

"But I don't know why! Why did it try to kill me?"

"Stella, the why doesn't matter. The only thing that matters is you're alive."

"The Ashcroft's are dead," I whisper.

"Which is sad, but it's not your fault. Do yourself a favor and let this go. Leave that house alone. It isn't your problem anymore."

"So, you won't help me, that's what you're saying," I say, standing up to leave.

"I'm saying I *can't* help you. I can't help anyone. I mean, look at me, Red," he says, gesturing around his living room. "I can't even help myself."

This time there's a tinge of sadness when he smiles. Gideon Gray is a broken man. I'm the one who broke him and I can't make that right. But I can still help the Ashcroft's, even without his help.

"I'll show myself out," I say.

He runs after me as I'm walking towards the car. "Promise me you won't go back to that house!"

I keep walking. I won't make a promise I can't keep.

The house looms over me the second time around. Its exterior casts long shadows which seem to stretch towards me, pulling me in. Or maybe it's the aftereffects of days of nightmares playing tricks with my mind. Either way, I'm about to let my guard down. I cut through the yellow tape sealing off the entrance and push the door wide.

The unlit hallway seems to be holding its breath, waiting for me. I didn't bother switching on the flashlight on my phone. The battery dies the moment I step on the porch and I don't want to see what's waiting for me in the dark. It felt braver, better, to surrender to it, to face it like this. To become a part of it. So I shuffle through the house, going slowly, feeling my way around the edges. Maybe this way it'll take longer for the spirit to know I'm here.

My hip bumps against an end table, sending a vase crashing to the floor. The sound rattles inside my rib cage, making my heart pound double as fear floods through me. I freeze, rooted to the spot. I could turn back. The light from outside still silhouettes the edges of the front door like a beacon of safety. I could still find my way out.

But then what would happen to the next people who moved in here? Would they end up like the Ashcroft's? If they did, could I live with the knowledge that I could've prevented it?

I force myself forward, feeling along the edges of the counters until I come to the next doorway. The basement. The door has been shut. Maybe by the police. Maybe by someone else. I grasp the handle, my sweaty hand slipping as I try to turn it.

Once I open the door I peer down into the darkness, climbing down the stairs again and turning on the light. This time I'm better prepared, thanks to Gideon's advice. I researched.

I pull the braided bundle of mugwort out of my bag and light the end. I read that it would work better than regular incense and since mugwort is used for protection, I hope it might help me. I wave the braid around as I walk, making sure to get in the corners.

"I don't know who you are or why you're here, but you need to move on. I won't let you stay here and hurt any more people."

The TVs click on, filling the room with the hiss of static.

Not again. I can't fight it. I don't know how. I brace myself for another run out of here.

"Stella! Are you here?"

It can't be. "Down here!" I call back.

Sure enough, Gideon appears at the top of the stairs. "You shouldn't be here. We need to leave."

"But—

"There isn't time to argue about this. I can explain after."

The TVs start switching off. I notice something gathering in the static snow of the screens before they do. Something like the outline of a person blocking the view. "You're here, aren't you?"

The temperature of the room drops until it's so cold I can see my breath. A hand touches the nape of my neck, phantom fingers wrapping around. I turn, waving the mugwort in the space in front of me. The smoke gathers in places, clinging to something.

"I said get out."

I scream, dropping the mugwort as I'm lifted off my feet. But it's not the spirit. It's Gideon. He throws me over his shoulder and sprints up the stairs. "What are you doing?" I shout at him.

"I'm saving our asses, Red. You're too stubborn to listen so I had to improvise."

"Put me down!"

"Why? So you can argue with the damned thing some more? That's not going to work."

We're in the kitchen now. There's just enough light coming in through the windows that I can see the fuzzy outline of the furniture. Gideon sets me down on my feet and places his hands on my shoulders.

"There's one thing that might, but when I say run this time, you have to run. Can you do that?"

I cross my arms, trying to stop shaking. "You're not going to sacrifice yourself, are you?"

"What do you take me for? I'm not some noble hero. Maybe just as stupid, though."

I watch as he kneels down and reaches behind the stove. There's a clanking sound and the pungent scent of gas lingers in the room. Gideon stands, coughing. He wraps a scarf around his mouth and nose.

"Now cover your mouth and run."

I do. I don't care about knocking things over as I race towards the light. I hear Gideon's footsteps thundering behind me.

We're going to make it.

Gideon shoves me from behind and I hit the porch face first. I get to my feet and turn around, anger running through me. "What the hell was that for?"

He doesn't answer. Gideon stands in the doorway with his back to me, arm outstretched, clasping something tightly in his gloved hands.

"They're mine," a voice hisses from somewhere inside the house. "They both belong to me."

"Go to hell," Gideon says.

A knot of dread builds in my stomach. I'd heard that voice before. The same voice whispered in my ear as it choked the life out of me. The voice from the basement.

I've been waiting for you, Stella.

"Can you see him?" My voice comes out in a hoarse squeak.

"Get away from the house," Gideon says.

"Not without you."

There's a sound that bellows through the walls. Something between a human shout and the roar of a wild animal. It's so loud it rumbles under my feet and shakes the windows.

"Get back," Gideon yells.

I see the flame a second before he tosses the match into the house. This time, I'm the one grabbing him, dragging him down the stairs as the house explodes.

Someone is singing. It takes me a minute to recognize the tune as "Have Yourself a Merry Little Christmas".

I groan.

Not more Christmas music. I must be in hell.

I definitely feel like it. Every part of me aches and my head has been replaced with a cinder block.

"Is my singing that bad? Hey! Hey, Red, are you with us? We need a nurse in here!"

I open my eyes. Gideon is half in, half out of a doorway, shouting. I look down and see an IV taped to my hand. I'm in the hospital. Again.

"You look funny," I mumble as Gideon sits in the chair next to me. I realize a moment later that the tube wrapped around his face is a cannula, a tiny tank is giving him oxygen. There's gauze on his neck and arms.

"First you complain about my singing and then you insult me. Gotta say, I'm not feeling the love."

"Don't sing Christmas music."

"Where's your Christmas spirit?"

"You're the Medium. You tell me."

"Are you always this grumpy when you wake up?"

"Usually she's worse." Kaelee appears in the doorway, her arms loaded with snacks. "I thought you might be hungry when you woke up. And I owe you."

A nurse is behind her. She checks my vitals and asks questions. "You two are lucky. That was a huge gas leak. They're saying there's nothing left of the house."

I look at Gideon. I can't say much in front of the nurse and Kaelee. "Are you okay?"

"Minor burns and bruises. Nothing to worry about," he says.

What he didn't say is that we're lucky to be alive. The doctor comes by after a while, and both Kaelee and Gideon leave to give me some privacy. The doctor says my head injury is the most concerning bit of my injuries, but waking up as soon as I did is a good sign. She recommends another day or two in the hospital so they can monitor me. I don't argue.

Kaelee has a lot of questions. She doesn't say anything, but I can tell from the looks she gives Gideon and me.

"What are you going to tell her?" he asks during one of his visits once she's left the room.

"I don't know. I just know it can't be the truth."

Gideon nods. "The fire destroyed the house and it should have destroyed the link between the house and the spirit."

"Should. Meaning you don't know for sure."

"Nothing in life is certain. We'll find out if and when they rebuild the house."

I still have questions too, and I can't wait any longer for answers. "Why did you go to the house? How did you know I would be there?"

Gideon clears his throat. "After you left, I had a feeling you were going to try again. I couldn't stop thinking about everything you told me, about the house and the people who lived there. I'd never dealt with malevolent spirits, but I knew other Mediums who had. I had a bad feeling about what you'd be going up against. So I started making calls. I started researching. Looking into the ownership and history of the house."

"What did you find?"

"Back in 1973, a man owned the house who was convicted of wrongful imprisonment and murder. I'll spare you the details, but they found a few bodies in the house. The basement was where he would torture his victims."

I shiver. "That's awful."

"I'll be honest with you, Stella. Other than being around the same age as his victims, I'm not sure why the spirit targeted you. Maybe it just wanted more victims. But that wasn't the feeling I got."

I think back to what CeeCee said. *This has nothing to do with her.*

"Gideon, there's something I haven't told you about the first attack. Something I don't know how to explain."

When I finish, Gideon doesn't say anything. I keep talking to fill the silence. "On the internet, which I know isn't the best source, they said she could be a doppelgänger. But if she's my doppelgänger, well, they said if I saw her, I'm going to die."

This grabs his attention. "You aren't going to die, Stella, despite all the close calls you've had lately."

"You're just saying that to make me feel better."

"Actually, I'm not. One of my *abilities* is I'm able to see when people are going to die," he says, an edge of disdain in his voice.

I didn't want to believe him, but it'd be impossible not to after everything I'd been through. Gideon didn't call me crazy after I told him everything about CeeCee, and he at least deserved the benefit of the doubt.

"Anybody? So you can tell me when I'm going to die?"

"Anybody. And not exactly. It's like an energy around people. I can see changes to their energy. Right now yours seems steady, if a bit less than normal. If I'm around people long enough, I get visions of how or when, which is why I don't spend much time around people anymore. It's a curse, knowing what I know."

"You said you don't anymore? So you had a family once?"

"I had a wife. One day, I had a vision. I knew she'd get sick. I knew she wasn't going to survive. I spent every day with her right until the end, but I tried to find ways to stop it. I reached out to people I knew for solutions. The one thing you can't fight is death. After, I focused on work, until…"

"Until me."

Gideon looks over at me. "It wasn't all you. I'd started drinking more. It dulled my abilities, it dulled the pain, but my work started to suffer. Clients were unhappy even before we met."

"But I was the one who ended things. I was the final nail in your coffin."

"Yup. After there was no more work for me. No more spirits. No more of other people's pain to cover up my own."

I've been so selfish. So stupid and careless. I'm different now. I have a chance to do things differently. "Before that house, I'd never seen a spirit, but now I'm seeing them all the time," I admit.

"Sometimes people are born with abilities but as they age into adulthood, they lose them because people in their life have taught them it isn't okay. So they shut them out. I think that might be what happened to you. Hospitals are always full of ghosts, so I'm not surprised it's easier for you here."

"What about CeeCee? If she's a spirit, why does she look like me? Why did she age?"

"I can't explain her, Stella. There are a lot more unexplainable things in this world than we think there are."

There's only one thing left to ask him. "I know I can't take back what I did, but I'd like to continue being Stella Winters. Only I want to do things right. Helping people, getting rid of malevolent spirits."

"You want to go legit?"

I nod. "But I also want you to work with me. There's so much I don't know that I can learn from you. I think we could help each other. Would you be willing to team up?"

Gideon regards me for a moment, mulling it over. "You know I can be a pain in the ass."

"I can be a bigger one."

"I'm also a functioning alcoholic."

"Functioning is debatable. We'll work on it."

He gives me one of his wry smiles. "You're on, Red."

JOLLY OLD SAINT RYAN

LAURA MORRISON

In retrospect, the odor should have been a dead giveaway. On the other hand, the smell of decaying flesh was not at all uncommon in his line of work. So many dead animals ended up in chimneys. When one's profession necessitates one stuffing oneself down most chimneys in the world, that translates to bumping up against more than one's fair share of rotting carcasses.

This one, though, was larger than most.

Much larger. By far the largest he'd ever dealt with.

Ryan knew almost immediately it was human, but for a few moments his horrified brain grasped for alternative explanations. A deer. A deer had somehow gotten into the house below, and in its panic at being confined had begun to jump about; it had leaped into the chimney, got wedged in, and died. And... the homeowners had...left it there? No. Well, then, it was a giant of a raccoon, grown vast due to hypothyroidism. But no, that wouldn't work either. No raccoon could get that big, plus, all the raccoon carcasses he'd found down chimneys before had been much furrier—even the super decomposed ones.

He registered his heart was hammering, and the cold sweat he'd broken out in was making it difficult to hold the bag of presents. With what remained of his senses, Ryan put a finger to the side of his nose and flew out of the chimney and onto the roof. Landing funny on his ankle, he fell onto the rough shingles with a cry of pain and a thud.

"Careful," grumbled Lila from the passenger seat of the sleigh. "This night's interminable enough already. If you're gonna be limping through the rest of it, it's gonna—" Lila focused on Ryan and stopped short. "What the hell, man?"

Ryan was on hands and knees, gasping, muttering, "No, no, no," under his breath, and shaking his head.

"Ryan," barked Lila. "What's wrong?" She was so concerned she even went so far as to set aside the book she'd been reading.

"I—I—" Ryan spluttered. "There's *a human body* down the chimney." He flapped an arm in the general direction of the chimney.

Lila scrunched up her nose. "Ew, gross." Her gaze flicked in the direction of the chimney, and she settled back into her seat.

"That's all you have to say?" Ryan snapped, pushing himself to his feet and glaring at the elf. "*Ew, gross?* I bet I have decayed person bits on my clothes. Decayed person bits."

"Yeah man, it's nasty. But—well—I mean, it happens."

Ryan blinked at Lila. "Huh? *It happens?*"

Lila nodded. "Duh. Happened to your predecessor twice. If he'd had a chance to teach you the ropes, I bet he'd have mentioned it, but well—he didn't really get a chance now, did he?"

"Don't you dare get into that," Ryan snapped. "Not right now." He took a steadying breath. "He found two bodies down chimneys?"

Lila nodded again. "Yeah, but he'd been Santa for like thirty years, so it's not like it's a common occurrence."

"But still—" Ryan spluttered. "Two murdered bodies in chimneys? How can you be so casual about such a thing?"

She raised her eyebrows and gave a little scoff. "Funny how quick your brain went to murder."

"Well, I mean… Why else would a body be stuffed up a chimney?"

She rolled her eyes at him. "Why do you assume someone stuffed it *up* the chimney? Probably some idiot just got stuck climbing *down*. Some drunk twenty-something guy on a dare? A particularly stupid thief?"

He rolled his eyes right back at her. "Lila, you've never been down a chimney, have you? No one would go down one if they didn't have to, or if they didn't have magic to assist them. Chimneys are nasty and filthy and sooty. I bet I'm gonna get lung cancer from this stupid job." He paused to clear his throat, which felt gritty all of a sudden. "Nope, the body was totally stuffed *up* the chimney by a murderer."

"Sure. Whatever. Your mind is a dark, dark place, Ryan."

He gave a slight shrug. There was no point arguing. "Be that as it may, I know I'm right. Get this: When I was going down the chimney, it wasn't just the body that stopped me. There was some sort of hard surface. Not the body. I thought it was the bottom of the chimney at first, but it wasn't. I was still halfway up the chimney when I stopped."

She narrowed her eyes. "I don't understand what you're saying."

He spelled out his suspicions for her, "I think someone stuffed the person up, and bricked over it or whatever to keep the smell out of the house. And to keep body parts falling down as it decayed."

"Whoa."

Ryan nodded. Then he shuddered, brought back to the reality of his situation by the smell of his clothes. He began to gingerly peel off the red suit, thankful he'd thought to pack a spare. "Toss me the extra, will you? It's in my backpack." As he waited, he adjusted the plain black t-shirt and gray sweatpants he'd worn as an extra layer since the red wool of the suit made him itch.

"What are you going to do about it?" Lila asked as she leaned down to pick up Ryan's backpack.

"The body? I dunno."

"Your predecessor would have known. He—"

"I already told you," Ryan snapped. "I don't want to talk about him. Not now."

"It's never the right time to talk about him, is it, Ryan?" Lila muttered as she opened up his backpack and began to rummage through the contents.

"Well, why should I talk about him?" he sighed, his gaze drifting back to the chimney.

"Because—unlike the rest of you—he wasn't too awful. I downright liked him sometimes. I miss him, and I want to talk about him."

She wadded up the suit and tossed it at him. He was so preoccupied with staring at the chimney, he didn't spot the suit in his periphery and it hit him in the side of the head.

He uttered his second yelp of the evening, shot her a glare, and said, "Well, I've apologized about a hundred times—literally—so I don't see what more you expect of me." He winced a bit as he pulled the left pant leg over his twisted ankle.

Lila sighed. "You're the worst. Like, literally."

"Whatever," he sighed as he shrugged into the red jacket and began to button it. "I'm not."

She shrugged.

Ryan took a few paces toward the chimney.

"What are you doing? You're dressed. Get in and let's get moving."

"No. Not yet."

"Don't tell me you're going back down the chimney."

"No. It's full of dead body."

"Well, not down the chimney. I mean through the door or a window. You're still delivering presents here? After what just happened?"

"Well, if there are kids here, yeah. Isn't there a sacred oath or some crap? Give the brats their toys. I made a promise to honor The List. And The List says there are kids here."

"Oh, come on. What is this? You trying to prove you're not the worst? Proving me wrong by walking into the house of a murderer to give some children a few toys they're gonna break in like two seconds—"

Ryan cut her off, "Even if the murderer's still living here, my magic will protect me."

"You know very well it isn't one hundred percent protection. How many times a year do you get discovered by people?"

"A lot," Ryan conceded. "But I'll be super careful here. Obviously."

"But a murderer's going to be on high alert. Obviously. I would imagine murderers are very light sleepers."

"Know what? It's so sweet you care, but shut up. I'm going down there."

She shot him a glare. "You know very well I don't care. Go on down and get killed."

"You're jaded for a Christmas elf."

"I promise you I wasn't jaded when Nick was still alive. And I wasn't even too jaded when your predecessor was in charge, either."

"Blah, blah, blah. Cry me a river, snowflake. Look. Zip it. I'm going to give the kids in this house some plastic crap like I promised I'd do when I signed on for this materialistic shitshow. While I'm down there, know what else I'm gonna do? I'm gonna double check to see if someone really did board up that body in the chimney, then I'm gonna call 911 and tell the cops. Because I am a good person, Lila. Wait, are we in the United States? Is 911 what I want?"

Lila shrugged.

"I'll figure it out."

Lila rolled her eyes. "You know the oath isn't legally binding, or magically binding, or anything. Nothing's going to happen to you if you have a good reason for skipping a house."

"Well, I'm going down there anyway. Some loser in this house left a body up a chimney, and it was disgusting, and I am gonna call the cops on him. No one treats Santa like that and gets away with it."

"Ah, so this is about revenge. Not the magic of Christmas."

"Yes, Lila. Yes. This is about revenge. I'd call 911 from right here if I could, but you elves are all," and here Ryan affected a high, squeaky voice, "'No, Ryan, you can't use a cell phone. You can't bring electronics on the oh-so-sacred Christmas Journey. Electronics disrupt the quantum mechanics and the magic whatevery-blah which makes your journey possible in one night.'"

She shot him a glare over her now opened book. "I mean, that is why you cannot bring a cell phone. Whatevery-blah, though? You seriously learned nothing from your class about how this night works?"

Ryan groaned. "You think I paid attention?"

"Most Santas do, Ryan. *Most* Santas think it's fascinating to finally get the explanations about how Santa can do all this in a single night."

"I'm not most Santas, sweetheart."

"Just get moving so we can go on to the next house."

He gave a salute he knew would irritate her, smirked when he saw her jaw clench in anger, and turned to try to figure out a way off the roof. The magic only worked for chimneys, so he had to settle for clambering down a big tree branch which was close enough to the roof for him to reach. The bottom branch was a good distance from the ground, and the drop from that height further damaged his already injured ankle, but as he began to circle the perimeter of the house looking for an ideal entrance, Ryan consoled himself the worst was over. Locked doors and security systems were no match for the magic of Christmas, after all.

He walked across the cement slab back patio adorned with one lone plastic folding chair and breezed through the sliding door like it wasn't locked and barred. Inside, he found himself in the living room, which was devoid of both a Christmas tree and any sort of seasonal décor. Ryan idly wondered whether murderers were—generally speaking—the types who made a big deal of holidays. He guessed probably not.

But was this person even a murderer?

Ryan walked up to the fireplace, which appeared as though it hadn't been used in ages. He crouched down, stuck his head in, and looked up. It was, of course, black. If he'd been allowed a cell phone, he could have just used the flashlight app, but no, he had to lean in, twist around, and reach into the fireplace. And sure enough, about an inch short of the full extent of his reach, Ryan felt a hard surface made of some kind of brick, blocking the passage. Someone had indeed walled a body up in the chimney.

Ryan removed himself from the fireplace and took a moment. *Wow. A murderer. For real. Okay.* Well, he'd just dump the presents, call the cops, and go.

Surveying the living room further, he noted this particular murderer not only didn't decorate for Christmas, he also did not really do any sort of decorating at all. The space was the sort of thrift store spartan which made Ryan cringe. After all, for the past three years he had been living in a place styled after a life-size gingerbread house—it was a bizarre sort of opulence, and the sparse soullessness of the house in which he now stood was quite jarring in comparison. His gaze flitted over the orangey-brown couch littered with crumbs from an empty pretzel bag, to the coffee table adorned with a few empty diet soda cans, to a midsize TV with a mess of gaming systems suffocating in a sea of wires at its base.

Having no Christmas tree to put the presents under, Ryan opened up the black bag he had slung over his shoulder and unceremoniously dumped the contents on the hardwood floor by the fireplace. Then, he set to work looking for a landline on the first floor. Statistically speaking, it was a fruitless search, but worth a shot. This murderer would not get away with making Jolly Old Saint Ryan get covered in corpse bits. This murderer would pay.

The ground floor of the house had a kitchen, bathroom, laundry room, a home office/weight room, and the living room he'd already seen. Stairs went up to where the bedrooms must be, and an open door under the staircase led to the basement. Ryan ascertained pretty quickly there was no landline, but he poked around on the ground floor a bit longer, just because he was curious about what kind of stuff a murderer had in his fridge, whether a murderer separated his whites and colors, and how clean a murderer kept his bathroom.

Only once he had finished nosing around the first floor did something awful occur to him. The realization stopped him dead in his tracks.

He had not seen one shred of evidence showing any children lived in the house.

For a few paralyzing seconds, Ryan grappled with the thought that the victim in the chimney might not have been an adult. But no, one fact he'd become painfully, disgustingly certain of down in the chimney was this: the body was a big one.

Well then, if there were no kids, then it probably meant a family had moved out and the murderer had moved in, and the elves in the record-keeping department had messed up The List. Ryan cursed them under his breath and clenched his teeth; if the record-keeping elves had been even minimally competent, then Ryan wouldn't have come to this house in the first place and the nightmare in the chimney wouldn't have happened.

And a murder would have gone unreported.

Ryan didn't really care overmuch about whether the murder went unreported. He mostly just wanted to get the jerk back for the disgusting trauma he had suffered in the chimney.

He sighed and took a few steps out of the kitchen and toward the staircase.

A sudden feeling of misgiving stole over him.

Even though the big, black boots he wore were magic and utterly soundless, and though the stupid red suit also had some sort of spell on it which was something akin to invisibility, there was still always a slight chance Ryan might be detected.

But no, it was fine. It would have to take something huge

for all the magic safeguards to fail. He'd have to make a really loud sound, and then the person would have to be looking straight at him in really good light. Not much else could get past the cloaking magic, which worked so well it brought flashbacks of him in high school sitting by Kyra Javid—invisible in plain sight.

Secure in the knowledge he'd be safe as long as he didn't yell at the top of his lungs under bright light in the direct line of sight of the murderer, Ryan ascended the stairs and found himself in a dark hallway with four closed doors. Securely cloaked in Santa Magic, he limped down the hall and opened each doors in turn; a very disorganized linen closet, a bathroom significantly messier than the one downstairs, a room full of cardboard boxes in various states of unpacking—which further cemented Ryan's assumption he was only in this house at all due to some stupid elf's clerical error—and the one bedroom.

From the doorway, Ryan stared at the shadowy form of the guy who had killed a person and stuffed the body up his chimney. Ryan could only make out a big, dark lump under a blanket. He reminded himself about his magic boots and stepped past the threshold. The guy's cell would be by his bedside for sure. Had to be. Everyone kept their cell by their bed.

Sure enough, there it was under a lamp, lying in a little pool of moonlight.

Right beside it was an honest-to-goodness gun.

Ryan leaped backward in alarm as though it was a rattlesnake or something.

The awkward motion twisted his already hurt ankle, and he cried out in pain as he slammed onto the floor with a thud.

The guy in the bed gave a snort and jerked awake, his hand flying to the gun.

With every fiber of his being, Ryan wanted to get up and run. But the magic should shield him if he stayed still and quiet. So, he forced himself not to move. From where he lay sprawled on the ground, he watched as the guy waved his gun around the room.

"Who's there?" the guy barked, his head turning left and right as he scanned the room for movement.

The guy reached for the light. Switched it on.

Ryan clenched his teeth and squeezed his eyes shut, sure he'd be seen. Sure the combo of the light shining on him and the guy's state of heightened alert would be enough to get past the magic. Sure in about a second he'd have a bullet in his brain.

But …

"Seriously. I know you're there," the guy said, his voice all macho but his eyes—Ryan noted through one eye he dared to open a crack—looking nervous.

To Ryan's horror, the guy threw off the blankets and readied to get out of bed.

Ever so carefully, his heart racing, Ryan began a slow roll toward the wall. Too fast and the guy would detect the motion and spot him; too slow and the guy would step on him.

The guy kicked his feet over the side of the bed.

Ryan rolled a bit faster.

The guy's gaze flicked to Ryan.

Ryan felt a stab of cold terror and froze.

But the guy just blinked, drew his eyebrows together, shook his head, looked at the dark doorway to the hall, and yelled, "Fair warning. I'm armed."

The second the guy looked at the doorway, Ryan had continued his torturous slow-motion roll, so when the guy finally did get to his feet and walk out of the room, he missed stepping on Ryan by inches.

Ryan shut his eyes and gave his body a few moments to calm down. Down the hall, he heard the guy yelling, "I've used this thing before loads of times, and I won't hesitate to use it on you. I'll blow your brains out!" Well at least he was now convinced they were indeed in the USA and it was indeed 911 he wanted to dial.

Once Ryan's legs had stopped feeling shaky from the fear, he got to his feet and limped to the cell phone. He picked it up and walked to the window, peering out to see whether it would be a viable escape option once he'd called the crime in. A glance told him a definite no. There were no trees to climb down, no gutters, no trellises. Straight below was the cement patio with the sad little lone folding chair. Not a hospitable surface to land on from one story up.

Up. Of course. Was he Santa or was he not? The roof. He directed his gaze to the edge of the roof above him. It was a few feet up. A difficult reach, but not impossible. Next, Ryan examined the window itself. It had a hinge on the right and opened in like a door. Well, that simplified things. Ryan pocketed the cell, figuring he'd call from the safety of the roof instead of from the bedroom. Then he opened the window and—after a bit of tugging and cursing under his breath—he removed the screen and tossed it unceremoniously onto the bed.

Ryan climbed out of the window, his feet on the bottom ledge and his hands gripping the top. "Lila?" he hissed into the night. "Lila?"

He waited a few moments, listening intently.

Nothing. Could she really not hear him? Or was she just ignoring him? Maybe she was coming, but were her shoes magic like his boots? He had no idea.

Ryan glanced over his shoulder at the door to the hallway, then dared yelling a bit louder. "Hey, Lila. Help! I—" He heard footsteps in the hallway. "Lila? Get over here now and—"

Movement from the doorway.

The guy was standing right there.

And he was staring at Ryan. For sure staring at him. Seeing right through the magic.

"Lila," Ryan yelled, panicking and trying to grab for the edge of the roof as though he could maybe attempt a pullup. "Lila—"

The guy curled his lip and strode across the floor to the window, gun held in front of him in a way which made Ryan sure he knew how to use it. "Get down," the guy growled.

Ryan stared at him, horrified. "You can see me?"

"Huh? Can I—huh?" The guy shook his head. "Get down now, or I'm gonna push you out the window and you're gonna crack your head open on the patio down there."

Shaking, Ryan did as he was told.

The guy gave him a sneer as he sized Ryan up from his red woolen hat to his shiny, black, magic boots. "What's a scrawny hipster Santa doing breaking into my house?"

"I—uh—" Ryan didn't know what to say. Instead, he stopped abruptly mid-sentence and decided to remain utterly still, hoping somehow the magic could again slip into place even though the guy had already seen past it and was staring right at him. He doubted very much it would work, but—

The guy blinked, looking confused, and for a moment stared straight through Ryan. "What the—" the guy muttered. But then, just as Ryan was about to breathe a cautious sigh of relief, the guy focused in on him again. "How the hell'd you disappear, Santa?" He gave Ryan an aggressive shove with his free hand.

"M-m-magic," Ryan heard his voice stutter before he'd even fully thought through what he was going to answer. He plunged on, "The—uh—the suit's magic."

"The what now?" the guy said as though Ryan was talking crazy.

Ryan swallowed hard and decided to try to go invisible again. He stood stock-still and shut his eyes.

"Santa. What the hell are you doing."

Ryan conceded this guy was now definitely far too aware of Ryan's presence for him to be able to slip into invisibility under his nose again. He opened his eyes. "Don't kill me."

"Santa, I'd be well within my rights to shoot you. You're an intruder on my property."

"Man, seriously, you can't shoot me. I'm Santa," Ryan tried, then blathered on with the first thing that popped into his head, "Think of the children."

The guy raised one eyebrow. "Oh yeah? You're the actual, real Santa, are you?"

Ryan nodded.

"And you're bringing me presents," the guy sneered. "Aw, you shouldn't have."

"I didn't. Did you buy this house recently? From someone with kids?"

"Uh … yeah …"

"And you don't have kids? No kids live here?"

"No."

"I knew it," Ryan muttered. "Damn elves." Ryan gritted his teeth, making a mental note to go yell at the record keeping elves if he didn't get shot here. If he could just get back to the North Pole, he'd throw a good tantrum and toss some stuff around. Crack a few candy cane striped chairs across some tables and frisbee some decorative wreaths into some elf faces. Realizing his mind had somehow managed to drift, Ryan refocused on the guy, who was in the middle of talking.

"—some sort of dare or something? Dress up as Santa, break into a house, steal something? Is this a prank?"

Ryan cleared his throat and contemplated just running with this idea the guy had supplied him with. Sure. A prank. This was just a Christmas prank. Who'd shoot a guy for just taking part in a little Christmas prank? "Uh …."

Are you one of Dalton's friends? This has Dalton's name all over it."

"Yes," Ryan said. "Yes. Dalton. Okay. You got me. Darn."

"You do realize Dalton knows very well I have a gun? Like, do you understand he knew you could have gotten accidentally shot here? Or did he just convince you to break in here and leave out the little detail about how you might get shot?"

"Er … Well … Yeah, he sorta did not mention you had a gun. But you know Dalton … he's a forgetful guy …"

The guy gave him a skeptical look. "Know what we're gonna do? We're gonna call Dalton."

Ryan felt a jolt of panic, but then remembered the guy's cell was in his pocket. "Yeah, go for it. Give Dalton a call."

The guy turned to grab his phone. "Damn it."

"What?" Ryan asked, trying for an innocent tone.

"My phone." He turned to face Ryan.

Ryan tried to look calm, while his mind spun out of control. *Oh no, he knows I stole his phone. He's going to take it back, and he's going to call Dalton, and Dalton won't know what's going on, and this guy's gonna shoot me, and—*

"I musta left it downstairs." With his gun, he pointed at the door. "Move, Santa."

"Um, no thanks. You go call Dalton. I'll wait here." *And I'll escape out the window while you search downstairs for your phone, which you won't find, because I have it.*

"You'll wait here, huh?" the guy asked, casting a blatant look at the window Ryan had been attempting to climb out of minutes before.

"Come on, I won't try it again—"

"I'm not asking, Santa." He made a jabbing motion which clearly said, *Get moving.*

Numb with panic—because eventually this guy would find out Ryan had the phone—he limped toward the door. Over his shoulder, he tried, "How about I search around up here, and you—"

"Keep on walking, Santa. One thing you need to know about me—I've always wanted an intruder to break in so I can shoot someone and be within my legal rights. So, don't test me."

"But you wouldn't shoot one of Dalton's buddies—"

"You think I give a damn about Dalton's *buddies*? I hate Dalton. Which you'd know if you knew Dalton."

They were about halfway down the dark hallway when the guy snapped in alarm, "What the hell? Where'd you go?"

Not stopping to think, Ryan darted away as well as he could with his hurt ankle.

The guy yelled something incoherent and rage-filled. Gunfire reverberated in the narrow space. Once. Twice. Three times.

Ryan felt a searing pain in his left arm. He'd been shot. Shot. His steps faltered as he tried to assess the situation, and his body's damage.

The guy yelled, unhinged, "Where are you?"

Ryan walked on with faltering steps, not daring to look back.

"You—you—disappeared," the guy yelled the obvious. "Wait—wait—what the hell? What? *What?* Your suit's really magic? You're really—no—you're actually *Santa?*"

Ryan felt a bizarre, panicky desire to laugh as he clutched at his bleeding, throbbing arm. He had *told* the guy the suit was magic. Though he was still too scared to look over his shoulder as he limped his way toward the stairs, he heard the guy start to open the other doors in the hall, probably hoping Ryan had somehow opened one of the doors, snuck in, and shut the door, all right under his nose—because that would make a lot more sense than believing Santa was real. It was funny the solutions a brain tried to dream up to explain away blatant magic. Ryan knew he shouldn't be so condescending about it, since three years ago he'd reacted the exact same way. Hell, he'd pretty much been in the exact same situation.

Ryan reached the top of the stairs and dared to look back down the hall. The guy was just shutting the linen closet. Then Ryan saw him reach out and touch a switch on the wall.

The hall was suddenly flooded with light.

The guy looked straight down the hall toward the stairs. Right in Ryan's direction. Right *at* Ryan. The guy raised his gun. Pointed it at Ryan. "Don't move an inch. We need to talk. This is insane." Then a flash of sudden panic spasmed across his face. Ryan could see him swallow a heavy swallow, even though they were a few yards apart. The guy asked slowly, cautiously, as though afraid of the answer, "How did you get in my house …?" He swallowed again. "Did you—uh—did you go down the … chimney?"

Ryan took a heavy swallow of his own. *Oh no.* He shook his head. He took a step backward.

And fell down the stairs.

The first thing Ryan was aware of was a splitting headache. Also, blackness. He opened his eyes, which fixed the second problem.

He blinked, disoriented. It took him a few moments, but everything which had transpired came rushing back. He looked down at his bloody, throbbing arm, finding it hard to process the fact he'd been shot. With his other hand, he examined the wound, gingerly. It looked like it had just grazed his skin, and there was no bullet lodged in him.

Figuring he'd better try to stop the flow of blood, he pulled off his red woolen hat with the stupid white pom-pom on the end and held it to the wound.

The injury taken care of as well as could be done for the moment, Ryan looked around.

He was definitely in a basement. The lack of windows and general damp, underground sort of feeling indicated as much. But this was not a torture chamber, and he had to admit the big leather couch he was sprawled on was pretty comfy. Across from him was a bookshelf, half filled with books and half filled with game boxes and figurines which looked to be of the sci-fi and fantasy persuasion. Ryan recognized almost all of it. He wasn't a sci-fi/fantasy fan himself, but he'd seen the stuff on the factory floors up at the North Pole when he'd done the obligatory walk-throughs a Santa had to do to mingle with the common elves and make them feel appreciated.

In the corner of the room Ryan could see without turning his aching head, he spotted a card table with four chairs around it. He thought he could discern a few dice scattered across the tabletop. Was the gun-toting murderer a D&D player? This did not track. Ryan wondered whether he'd been brought to a different house while he'd been unconscious. But then, why couldn't a gun-toting murderer have dorky hobbies? It wasn't like all the guy did was murder people.

Ryan shifted to find a more comfortable position than the one his unconscious body had fallen into when it'd been tossed onto the couch.

"You're awake?" asked a voice from somewhere behind him.

Ryan swallowed, cleared his throat. "Where are we?"

"My basement. I had to carry you down, Santa."

"How long was I unconscious?" *And why is Lila not checking on me?*

"Just a few minutes." The guy walked around the couch and sat on the armrest, looking at Ryan with narrowed eyes. "While you were lying there, you went invisible again."

"I told you, the suit's magic."

"You *cannot* mean you're really Santa."

"I do mean I'm really Santa."

"*The* Santa?"

"Well … yeah … But probably not Santa like in the same way you think of when you think of Santa." Was he really saying this to another living creature who wasn't an elf? Yes. Yes, he was. Because this dude wouldn't kill Santa. It would take an exceptionally messed up person to off Santa Claus.

"Oh yeah? How so?"

Ryan cleared his throat. "The real Santa died ages back. He wasn't some immortal forever young—or forever old, I guess—being. He was just a guy who met some elves—and yeah, elves are a thing—and, okay, wow I don't even know where to begin with how to explain this crap."

The guy rested his gun on his knee, holding it loosely. He studied Ryan. "Elves are real?" His gaze flicked to his bookshelf and card table. "Are they tiny and squeaky, or are they cool?"

Ryan blinked at him. *Neither.* "Uh … They're kinda people-ish. Not the little squeaky-voice things from *Rudolph*. I guess they're a lot more like the Dungeons and Dragons kind.

Actually, no," he amended, "they're more Lord of the Rings, because they don't really seem to die. They're always talking about what it was like when the first Santa—the *real* Santa—was around, a long time ago. They're obsessed with his memory. It's creepy. Like a cult."

"How'd you end up as Santa?"

Not wanting to give the guy with a gun any ideas, Ryan answered vaguely, "The torch got passed to me from the previous Santa."

"So—like—you were the previous Santa's apprentice or something?"

Ryan tilted his head to the side. "Eh, sorta? The suit gets passed on from one Santa to the next when one retires—or dies, or whatever."

The guy scooted off the arm of the couch and sat down on it, apparently making himself comfortable for a chat. He leaned toward Ryan with one arm on a knee. "What does a Santa do when they retire?"

"Um …" Ryan shrugged, sending a spasm of pain through his wounded arm.

The guy registered Ryan's wince, but didn't ask about the pain, or acknowledge it in any way. He just pushed on asking about Santa stuff. "Didn't the Santa before you tell you his plans for retirement?"

Ryan shook his head. "Nope. No, he did not."

The guy gave him a curious look. "How did the topic of his retirement not come up?"

"It just didn't," Ryan snapped.

"Geez," the guy said, offended, leaning back. "Excuse me for being curious. It's not every day a person gets to talk to the real Santa."

Ryan gave him a skeptical look. "You actually believe me?"

The guy shrugged, then nodded. Then he shrugged again. "Well …" he waved a hand at Ryan's suit, "the magic outfit is pretty convincing. People don't just go and disappear in front of someone's eyes. And if magic is a thing, and since it is the night before Christmas, and since you are dressed like Santa, and you were trying to climb onto my roof…"

As soon as the guy mentioned the roof, Ryan's thoughts leaped to the chimney, and to the realization the guy had appeared to have had right before Ryan had fallen down the stairs.

The guy's mind seemed to have made the same leap. Ryan saw the moment the guy's body tensed; saw his grip on the gun tighten; saw his eyes grow wary.

Their conversation about elves and magic suits screeched to a halt, replaced by a very charged silence. Ryan had no idea what to say; no idea how to get out of this if Lila wasn't going to come and rescue him. He looked toward the stairs which led up to the first floor, and wondered whether the door was locked. Probably it was. So in the unlikely event Lila would be bothered to put down her book and come check on him, she wouldn't even be able to get into the basement—she couldn't walk through locked doors like he could.

Ryan sighed, and shifted uncomfortably.

He felt a weight in his pocket.

He still had the guy's phone. Somehow, it hadn't fallen out when he'd careened down the staircase. He broke the charged silence with, "Can I use the bathroom?" just as the guy said—

"How did you get in my house?" He blinked, then answered Ryan's question with a curt, "No, you can't."

"But I need to pee."

"You can wait. Answer my question." He looked down at the gun in his hand, then slowly back up at Ryan, all significant and threatening.

Ryan wanted to snap at him, "I get the point. Yes, you have a gun." But instead he took a breath, pushed the Santa hat more firmly onto his bleeding wound, and said, "I walked through the sliding door, man." He could feel himself breaking out in a sweat. He hoped the guy wouldn't notice and take it to mean Ryan was lying. The thought made him sweat all the more. And worse: it wasn't really too much of a lie anyway. He *had* walked through the sliding door. Never mind he'd only done it after finding the body in the chimney.

"No, you didn't. You didn't use the sliding door. I have a security alarm. It didn't go off." The guy got to his feet and walked over to Ryan. "Why are you lying to me? Why won't you tell me if you went down the chimney?" From where he stood over Ryan, he pointed the gun right at him.

Ryan pushed back into the cushions, as far as he could get from the gun. He said, "It's the magic suit. The thing's made to get past security. If Santa couldn't get past security systems, every Christmas everyone's alarms would be going crazy all over the world. I'm telling you, I walked right through the door."

The guy studied Ryan intently for a few moments, then backed off a few steps and lowered the gun to his side. "The suit gets past security systems?"

Ryan nodded. "Yes. It does. Want me to show you?"

The guy shook his head. He looked Ryan up and down. "No. I want to try it myself."

Ryan felt a chill. "No. This is my suit. I'm *Santa*. You can't just—put it on." He shook his head and found himself wrapping his good arm around his torso, hugging the suit to himself. If this guy put the suit on, the Santa torch would pass to him. The magic would leave Ryan, never to return. It was a one-time deal.

The guy said, "Well, I'm the one with the gun, and I want to try it on."

Ryan shook his head. "You can't." *This is not happening. No.*

The guy took three fast strides forward and held his gun right against Ryan's forehead.

Ryan leaned back as far as he could go, but the guy just pushed the gun right along with him. The guy said, "Sounds like you've got a pretty sweet gig. Magic suit makes you invisible and bypasses security systems, magic sleigh takes you to the North Pole where you can hide out all year long from the cops who will one day inevitably find you have killed your wife and hid her body in your chimney."

With those words, Ryan knew his fate was sealed. No one admits to murder and lets the person they told walk off unharmed. Ryan tried to talk, found his voice wasn't working right, cleared his throat, and tried again. "No. It doesn't work like that," he lied. "You can't just put it on and the magic just transfers from me to you. There's—uh—there's a ritual the elves have to perform. A—"

"You know what? I am willing to give it a try and see what happens anyway."

"But—" Ryan gasped. "But—no—"

The guy cut off Ryan's blathering, "Know what, Santa? I find it interesting I just told you I stuck my wife's body up the chimney, and you didn't bat an eyelash. Didn't exclaim or freak out or anything. Almost like you already knew about the body."

Crap. Crap. Crap. "I—uh—I—"

"Yeah. Uh huh. You did go down the chimney."

Ryan stared at the guy, feeling suddenly all floaty and sur-real. He realized he was literally staring down the barrel of a gun. It almost made him laugh.

"Take off the suit."

Ryan shook his head.

The guy cocked the gun.

"You do not want to put this thing on."

"Yes. I do."

"Please. Hear me out. Don't shoot me."

The guy heaved a sigh. "Fine. Talk. You're not going to change my mind. But talk if you must."

Ryan swallowed, then said in a rush, "Look, if you put on the suit, then you do become Santa. Like the magic passes from me to you, and you turn into Santa. And I swear, you may be thinking it'd be awesome—you're thinking the suit would be an awesome way to bypass security and rob a bunch of banks or something and get rich, right?"

The guy shrugged, then nodded.

"Well, dude, listen. It does not work that way. I was in your shoes three years ago. I was having probably the exact same thoughts you're having. But the magic this thing comes with has all sorts of strings attached. Like—believe me about this—the magic only works on the night before Christmas. I swear."

"Yeah, right. Sure."

"No. I promise. I swear on my life. It's true. I didn't believe it either when the Santa before me told me. I thought he was just trying to talk me out of—uh—taking the suit. But it is *true*."

"I'm gonna go ahead and take the risk."

"One more thing. When you have the suit on, you can't—"

"Shut up."

"But—"

"I said shut up."

Ryan sighed and slumped into the couch. "I didn't convince you?" Of course he hadn't convinced the guy. Just like the Santa before Ryan hadn't convinced him.

The guy shook his head and cocked the gun again in lieu of words.

"Okay," he gasped, throwing his hands up in the air in some random, ineffectual gesture of self-defense. "Okay. Just give me a change of clothes and I'll—"

"Take it off here."

"No." Ryan needed to use the phone in his pocket. He needed to. "No. I can't get undressed in front of you. It makes me uncomfortable."

"Do it."

"Are you gonna kill me?"

"Honestly, Santa, yeah. I think I am."

Ryan blinked a few times, swallowed heavily, internally cursed out karma for being every bit as awful as people said, and asked, "Then can you give me this one last request?"

"Your last request is to change out of your Santa suit in private?"

Ryan nodded.

The guy sighed. "Fine. Come on."

Back on the first floor, the guy led Ryan to the laundry room Ryan had already poked around in and told him to go through the dryer to find some clothes to change into.

"Hurry up," the guy snapped.

Ryan jumped, and picked up the pace. He grabbed a green t-shirt and some gray track pants with a red stripe, then looked around at the guy. "Okay. Where do I change? In here?"

"Not the green shirt. I like it. I don't want holes in it."

Ryan stopped to stare at him.

"Get a different shirt."

"Okay." Ryan rummaged through the dryer for a different shirt. "This one okay?" He held up a faded old Dave Matthews Band tour shirt.

"Yeah. Sure."

"Can I change in here?"

The guy nodded. "Just hurry up." He turned and was about to walk out the door when Ryan decided to attempt one last try at talking this guy out of it—

"Wait."

The guy groaned and turned. "What."

"You *really* don't want to do this. Look, you may think you comprehend the meaning of boredom, but you have no idea. None at all. Not until you are Santa on Christmas Eve. Ever wonder how Santa hits all the houses in one night?"

"No. Because I always thought Santa wasn't real, idiot."

"Fair. Okay. Well consider it now. How does Santa deliver presents all over the planet?"

"Uh, gee, I don't know … Magic?" the guy asked in a bored voice.

"Yes. Magic. Magic which messes with all sorts of quantum physics and stuff. It makes this mystical time bubble around the suit and the sleigh and the reindeer and the dumb, awful, cynical elf who accompanies Santa, and I am telling you Christmas Eve stretches out into one hellish torment of torture. There's no way to measure how long it is, but Christmas Eve feels like it goes on for a year. At least. Fly to a house, go down a chimney, breathe in soot, deliver presents, go up the chimney, rinse and repeat, and repeat, and repeat, and repeat."

"Better than prison, though, eh?" was all the guy came back with as he leaned against the doorframe and lazily pointed the gun at Ryan.

"I don't know, man. Honestly, I don't know if it is. Every year, about halfway through Christmas Eve, I start to believe in God again. Because I think I am in Hell. Not only is it just an interminable nightmare of repetition, but also there are the people. So many people. You'd think with this magic suit, and since I come at nighttime, not many people would find me, but they do. Like kids waiting up for Santa, and parents with insomnia, and whatever. And you always gotta talk to them. With the kids, you gotta be all jolly and ho-ho-ho and shit. And with the adults, you gotta convince them they're not insane. Every damn conversation you have adds time to the journey, and I am telling you it is not worth it. Sure, you get to spend the rest of the year safe at the North Pole, but—" Ryan stopped short, wondering why on earth he'd finished on a positive note.

The guy nodded. "Yeah. That's the part I like. The part where the cops can't find me."

"Come on—"

"We're done. This conversation is done. Change."

"But—"

"You have one minute."

"No."

The guy slammed the door in his face. Conversation over.

Ryan listened for footsteps walking away. There were none. The guy must be standing right on the other side of the door. Well, Ryan would just have to whisper then. He took a steadying breath, gave the door a quick glance, and with shaking hands pulled the phone out of his pocket. He turned it on. He hit the word "emergency" on the screen, and he dialed.

The ringing in his ear made him jump. It was so loud. So, so loud. Frantically, cursing under his breath, he jabbed at the volume buttons on the side of the phone.

"Hurry up in there," the guy yelled.

"Sorry," Ryan called. "Sorry. You know, it's a little difficult taking off a shirt when you've just been shot in the arm!"

"Don't get sarcastic with me, Santa."

"I'll say whatever I damn please if you're gonna kill me anyway." It was then he realized the 911 dispatcher had picked up. "Can you track my location if I don't know the address I'm at? There's a guy trying to kill me—"

The dispatcher responded, but Ryan couldn't make out his words over the yell from the other side of the door, "Santa, are you whispering in there?"

Ryan nearly dropped the phone. He stared at the door. "Who, me?" he managed in a strangled gasp.

"Yes, Santa. You."

"No, I'm not whispering."

"Yes, you are."

"Fine, I am. I was praying, okay?"

"Were not."

"Was so."

"Santa, do you have a phone in there?"

"No."

"I'm coming in."

The doorknob turned. Ryan lunged at the door and pushed it back, but the guy was strong. Ryan recalled the weightlifting setup he'd seen in the guy's home office. At the time, he'd assumed the guy was like most people who had weights and didn't use them. He had assumed wrong.

"I can just shoot you through the door, idiot," the guy roared.

"If you damage the suit too much, it stops working," Ryan

lied. It struck him as a horribly stupid lie, but the guy seemed to buy it. At least, there was no gunfire. But Ryan would not be able to hold the door much longer. He looked down at the phone in his hand. He needed both hands if he was going to have any hope of keeping the door shut. He could still hear the dispatcher talking. Ryan said into the phone, "Please. Send help," then he tossed it, still on, into the open dryer. A few seconds later, the strain of holding the door closed became too much for his wounded arm. The guy exploded into the room in a fit of rage and rounded on Ryan.

On the roof, Lila was distracted from her book by the sound of sirens. She tried to focus back on the book, but the sirens kept getting louder and louder. When cars with flashing lights started to roll down the street the house was on, she finally gave up and tossed the book aside.

She walked to the edge of the roof and looked down, grumbling angrily in Elvish under her breath when the cars pulled to a stop in the driveway of the house she was standing on top of. She grumbled a bit more as she watched cops jumping out of their cars, barricading themselves behind open doors, and pulling out guns.

Then, she walked to the other side of the house and searched the shadows, certain of what she was going to see—and sure enough, there he was, a man in a red Santa suit trying ineffectually to run, but looking like he was being held back by an invisible tether.

She sighed, got into the sleigh, cracked the whip to wake up the dozing reindeer, and flew off, landing in the back yard behind the guy who—once the sleigh had moved—was now able to run a little further. When Lila yelled, "When you're wearing the suit, you can only go thirty yards from the sleigh," he stopped short and turned, waving a gun at her. She rolled her eyes and snapped, "Just get in the sleigh."

He shook his head. "No way. I am not getting in there."

She sighed. "You put on the suit. You're Santa. Get in the sleigh."

He looked past her with alarm on his face and ducked behind a bush.

She turned and looked behind her. Five cops were fanning out across the yard, facing the house.

"They can't see you. They can't see me or the sleigh either. Didn't he tell you anything before you—uh— Did you kill him?"

"I don't want to talk about it."

She frowned. "Great. Just great. Exactly what I did not need right now. Not only training another rookie Santa, but also, he's a murder. Yet another awful, murdering Santa. You have no idea how many horrible guys have met Santas through the years and offed them so they could take over and run from their lives." She looked away from him and stared at the reindeer, muttering, "Wayne the drug dealer. Ken the mafia boss. Darryl the stalker—man, was a stalker a good fit for Santa. And the list goes on." She turned back to him and contemplated him for a moment. "Just get in."

"I was kinda hoping I could just … uh … take the magic suit and run …"

She gave a snort of a laugh. "Thirty yards, man. Didn't the other Santa tell you?"

"No. He didn't." The guy gave her an angry stare, then with a giant sigh he got out from behind the bush and climbed into the sleigh. "I'm not saying I'm doing this thing. I'm just getting in this sleigh so we can talk easier."

"Cool, cool. Whatever. Come on, let's go to the next house." She started the reindeer moving and they took off into the air.

The guy gave a gasp of alarm and grabbed the edge of his seat. He stared at the rapidly receding ground, and asked over his shoulder, "Can't I just forego this Santa thing and just—"

"Just take the suit and go live a life of crime?"

He nodded.

"Sorry, kid. It only works on Christmas Eve. Didn't Ryan tell you anything?"

"I thought he was lying," the guy mumbled.

She shook her head. "They always think it's a lie …"

"It's really true?"

She nodded. "You took the suit. You're stuck. You don't want the gig, go foist the suit on one of those cops back there and make it his problem. But if you want a surefire way of avoiding getting charged for the murder back there, you become Santa."

He sighed and sat stone still for about two minutes, during which time she landed the sleigh on the next house, turned, and stared at him. Finally, he groaned, "Fine. Fine, I'll do it."

She nodded. "I know. It's a lot to process. You are going to be so, so bored by the end of this. But hey, it's better than prison." She gave him a few more seconds to process, then snapped, "Okay. Move. Take the bag and get down the chimney and give some kids some presents."

"But it's empt—" he started, then looked down at the bag he'd taken off the body along with the red suit. It was full again.

"Magic, man. You'll get used to it. Now go." Lila pointed at the chimney.

With a weary sigh, Santa got out of the sleigh and trudged to the chimney.

ACKNOWLEDGEMENTS

SAM HOOKER

This story wouldn't have been possible without the literary fiends at Black Spot Books demanding that I come out of my pillow fort and write a story. Now that it's done, I'm hanging a "do not disturb" sign on one of the load-bearing cushions of said pillow fort. It applies to anyone not bearing Fruit Roll-Ups.

DALENA STORM

I would like to thank Askold Melnyczuk and Paul Yoon for giving me feedback on a much earlier draft of this story, as well as the whole Bennington community for listening to me read a revised version as part of my thesis. Thank you also to my husband, JJ, for your final-round edits.

TIFFANY MEURET

Thank you to Lindy Ryan and the Black Spot Team for putting this together, as well as the other editors and contributors who made this anthology possible. I am honored to be included.

ACKNOWLEDGEMENTS

N.J. EMBER

There are many people I'd love to thank, but there's definitely a few people without whose support this story wouldn't have been possible. Thank you to Papa, Mom, Ginger, Amir, Rai, Tabbi, Areya, Eli, Amy, Tina and Raina for always believing in me. Thank you to my siblings for your love and encouragement. Finally, thank you to Monique Snyman, Lindy Ryan, and the rest of the Black Spot Books family.

LAURA MORRISON

Thanks to my mom and dad for the idea, and to Jennifer Flath for being the amazing beta reader you always are.

ABOUT THE AUTHORS

SAM HOOKER Legend has it that Sam Hooker writes from a cave in Antarctica by the light of the full moon, because the truth doesn't make for much of a legend. He lives in Southern California with his wife, Shelly, and son, Jack.

CASSONDRA WINDWALKER is a poet, essayist, and novelist presently writing full-time from the southern Alaskan coast. Her published works can be found in bookstores and online. She welcomes discussions with readers across social media.

DALENA STORM is a writer and educator living in Williamstown, MA. She holds a BA from Williams College and an MFA from Bennington. Her travels throughout Europe and Asia, and her study of religion, influence much of her writing.

DANIEL BUELL is a New Jersey-born booklover, foodie, and writer. When he is not in the kitchen making new recipes, he is building fantastical worlds and stuck in good book or two.

ALCY LEYVA is a Bronx-born writer who received his MFA in Fiction from The New School. His first two books, And Then There Were Crows and And Then There Were Dragons, are part of his Shades of Hell trilogy. He's pretty sure whoever wrote 2020 needs an editor.

TIFFANY MEURET is a writer hailing from Phoenix, Arizona. Her work has appeared in multiple publications, and her debut novel, A Flood of Posies, will be released in February 2021 from Black Spot Books.

N.J. EMBER is a paranormal fiction author who loves to write stories about survival and triumph over adversity. She currently lives in Michigan with her grandpa and a forever growingcollection of books and Funko Pop! figures.

LAURA MORRISON is the author of the fantasy realism novella Come Back to the Swamp, the sci-fi novel Grimbargo, and the young adult fantasy series, The Chronicles of Fritillary. She is also the writer of, and a voice actor in, the podcast Space Mantis, a spinoff of Come Back to the Swamp. She lives in the Metro Detroit area with her husband, two daughters, two cats, lots of bees, one vegetable garden, and sometimes neonatal foster kittens.

OTHER TITLES FROM BLACK SPOT BOOKS